OPERATOR 5:
THE SUICIDE BATTALION

SECRET SERVICE OPERATOR #5™

AMERICA'S UNDERCOVER ACE

THE SUICIDE BATTALION

By Curtis Steele

POPULAR PUBLICATIONS • 2023

PUBLISHING HISTORY

"The Suicide Battalion" originally appeared in the July/August, 1938 (Vol. 10, No. 4) issue of *Operator #5* magazine. Copyright © 2023 by Argosy Communications, Inc. All rights reserved.

CHAPTER 1
BLOOD SUCKERS

S LOWLY THE long freight train snaked its way across a countryside still desolate and deeply scarred by the heel of the invader. Farmhouses burned to foundations, villages and towns leveled to the ground, roads torn up, bridges, aqueducts demolished—on every side lay evidences of the ruthless destruction that had devastated the length and breadth of four great American states and turned them back into a wilderness.

North and South Dakota, Minnesota and Wisconsin had fared worse than the rest of the United States during the terrible years of the Purple Invasion. The final stronghold of the Mongol war-lord, Shan Hi Mung, this territory had been utterly ravaged as his sullen horde retreated into Canada. Sacked and pillaged, now scarcely a building remained standing.

But once more American pioneers were pressing into the war-torn wilderness, reclaiming it. As the train rolled through towns that were rising phoenix-like from their own ashes, the builders stopped their labor and stared. Railroad trains were still a strange sight after nearly four years of a conflict that had swept America bare of all modern comforts and civilized conveniences.

The nation had been feverishly rebuilding, fighting against time for fear its stark helplessness might lay it open once more to invasion from its powerful European rivals, now freed from the yoke of the Purple Empire and again returned to their ancient

scheming and grasping. Midway, that rebuilding had been halted by a revolt that threatened to thrust the country beneath the thumb of a despotic dictator. But in the nine months since the death of Frederic Blaintree, and the collapse of his rebel-

Open-mouthed, the crowd gaped up at the window!

lion, the forty-eight states had been reunited, tied together once more with strands of telegraph wire and the gleaming steel of transcontinental railroad tracks.

This gigantic task had owed much of its success to the broad vision and the untiring energy of a flashing-eyed, square-jawed, deceptively youthful-looking man in Washington listed on the roster of his country's Intelligence Service simply as Operator 5....

Men and boys waved at the passing train. Little did they suspect that the dungaree-clad figures in the doorways and clinging to hand-rails were not the trainmen they appeared but watchful soldiers—or that the slim youth, making his way over the top of the box-cars to the engine, was one whom the generals of the late Emperor Rudolph had done their utmost to trap.

Tim Donovan had been kicking his heels in the caboose for hours. He turned restlessly from the window and faced the other two dungareed occupants of the swaying car.

"Jimmy says the railroads are the life blood of the nation"— he yawned—"but it looks as if we're switched off onto a dead limb. Two weeks of rolling along like this—and not a thing happens. Four trains without as much as a hotbox to relieve the monotony—"

"Run along up to the engine." One of the others smiled at him—a dark-eyed figure whose feminine charms were poorly concealed by the rough clothing or the cap pulled down over her chestnut bob. "Maybe Peters will let you take the throttle."

"Okay, Di." Tim's freckled face twisted into a grin, and he accepted the suggestion with alacrity.

"It *has* been quiet," Diane Elliot said thoughtfully as soon as young Donovan had left. "Too quiet, Captain Howard. It worries me. In the month before your men were assigned to this duty, three trains were held up and looted on this route. Since we have been here there hasn't been even a sign of interference—which makes me believe that whoever has been preying upon our supplies knows that the trains are now guarded. Somewhere between here and Washington there has been a leak—"

Suddenly she stopped, lips half open, staring at a distant butte where the outline of a horseman had been briefly etched, then blotted out.

"What is it, Miss Elliot?" The young officer moved to her side.

"They know we are here—and we are being watched," Diane said firmly. "Now I *know* I am not mistaken. That's the third time I've seen a rider watching us from the hills—a rider who sped away the moment he had had a chance to look the train over. The other trains have been allowed to pass deliberately—but they know what we are carrying. They know how important it is that these supplies go through. This is the load for which they have been waiting."

"I am going out to pass the word." Captain Howard started for the door quickly. "If there is to be trouble, it must come soon—we are only three or four hours from the Line."

Diane's pulses were hammering as she pressed close to the window and watched for a further glimpse of that vanished horseman. They were only three or four hours from the Ferrara Line, America's bulwark against the pillaging armies that still roamed over helpless Canada.

FROM THE Great Lakes to Vancouver that line stretched a long string of entrenchments, concrete pillbox machine-gun turrets, underground galleries, barbed-wire entanglements.

General Sylvester Ferrara had supervised its construction and manned it—but again, it was Jimmy Christopher, Operator 5 of American Intelligence, to whom the nation was indebted for conceiving it and insisting that no effort be spared until the task of erecting it was completed.

For the first time in history the wide international border, that had so long been without any sign of fortification, was girded with steel and concrete from end to end. This was not against the good neighbors who once had dwelled to our north, only as a barrier against the savage despoilers who had subjugated the Canadian people. The Dominion of Canada was a wasteland, an open door for any invader who had designs upon the United States—with only the Ferrara Line to bar the way.

And now the Line was in danger!

Three trainloads of supplies, bound to the fortifications from Chicago, had been waylaid and looted in the wasteland of North Dakota. At first the depredations had been attributed to the lawless bands that infested the despoiled territory. Then, gradually, it had become apparent that there was something more than mere highway robbery behind this campaign of hold-ups.

This railroad line was a vital artery carrying the blood stream of the nation, and must be protected at any cost. Unable to tear himself away from the multitudinous duties which kept him in Washington, Operator 5 reluctantly had passed the task of investigating these robberies to Diane and Tim, two members of the devoted little band who had served him and their country so faithfully during the dark days of the invasion.

The train had dipped down into a wooded valley, was passing

through a spindly forest, coming out at its farther end and was swinging around a sharp curve—when the brakes went on with a suddenness that sent Diane spinning from the window and flung her against the front end of the car.

For an instant there was silence—silence that still echoed the squeal of wheels, clank of couplings. Then a terrific explosion sounded up at the head of the train.

At the same moment, the long line of cars rattled and shook from end to end—then started slowly backward as the engine went into reverse.

Peters had run into trouble, either a hold-up or a blockade—and was trying to run, to back out of it!

Diane had reached the back door of the caboose when there came another crashing explosion—this time almost on top of her. The earth trembled and the tiny car windows were shattered into splinters. Through the partly open door, she saw two tall trees toppling and bowing, as if to greet each other, as they crashed simultaneously to the right-of-way and interlaced over the track.

And then the caboose was rolling into them—crashing through their branches and finally groaning to a forced stop.

The trap was closed—and out from among the trees now rode dozens of black-masked horsemen. They were joined by others who came riding from the front end of the train. Like Western train-robbers, they raced up and down the cars, raining lead into every doorway, into every cranny from which a defender's gun barked. There must have been hundreds of them, Diane marveled, as she hurried through the front door of the caboose and climbed onto the freight car ahead.

QUICKLY, SHE pushed the door open and slipped inside, drew it shut behind her and climbed up on a pile of packing-cases to one near the roof. It was situated so that she could lift the top and crawl inside, then draw the cover down over her, bring the nails back into place, hammer in a few additional ones from the inside—and be securely hidden in a shipment of army rifles.

But just as she was about to step into the aperture she tensed, listened. That was not the crack of revolvers or automatics, but heavier—the boom of explosives more powerful than cartridges. Deep, reverberating booms—and then the crash of splintering wood.

From the edge of the door she peered out. The meaning of that bombardment became all too clear. Instead of depending on their firearms, these modern highwaymen were pelting the freight cars with hand grenades! The doors were being blown to pieces, the soldiers behind them killed or forced out into the open—then cut down mercilessly! Like leeches, the black-masked killers were swarming over the cars, shooting down the defenders. Already trucks and pack-trains were ranging up at the doors, being loaded with the looted supplies. The whole thing clicked off without the slightest hitch—and now Diane knew that there *had* been a leak! The carefully guarded secret of this shipment had been betrayed to these blood-suckers now out to sap the strength so vital to their weak, struggling country. They had known when the train was due, just where the soldiers were stationed, exactly which cars contained the most important shipments. Hard-eyed, Diane looked out at that slaughter. Her trigger-finger pressed longingly on the revolver clutched in her cold palm.

Before they could reach her she could bring down at least half a dozen of those thieving murderers. However, her orders were strict. She was to hide in that case of rifles and lie still until the case was taken from the car and delivered to its destination. Then would come her chance to go into action, if anyone tried to stop her from escaping with the information that would bring avenging troops down on these pillaging traitors!

Reluctantly, she started back toward her covert as a dozen riders galloped up beside the door of her car and began to dismount.

"Wait a minute—better not take any chances!" one of them shouted a warning to his fellows. His arm whipped back with a grenade from which he had drawn the pin.

The grenade arced forward quickly and slapped against the door with a terrific crash—just as Captain Howard and a dozen of his men came running along the side of the train and flung themselves forward in a gallant but hopeless charge. Bullets poured into them, hammered them down mercilessly. With a yell of fierce anger on his dying lips, Howard sank to his knees, staggered back to his feet—and then went down for the last time, sieved by a dozen lead slugs.

That much Diane saw as the force of the blinding explosion hurled her back into the interior of the car. Dazed, groggy, she scrambled up to her hiding-place, was half in the case before the cloud of smoke had thinned in the battered doorway. Automatically, she dropped back into place and drew the cover down, just as Captain Howard's death scream stabbed into her ears—echoed by a cry of mad fury that caught her up short and shook her out of the coma that held her half-stupefied. That voice could only belong to....

THE RESTLESS boredom which had irked young Tim Donovan disappeared the moment he stepped from the caboose and climbed to the catwalk on top of the freight car ahead. His show of indifference had been entirely for Diane Elliot's benefit—so that she would not sense and be alarmed by the uneasiness that tugged at him.

Like a blooded hound on the trail, Tim scented trouble. His nerves were atingle with warning, his alert eyes missed no detail of the passing scene as he worked his way forward.

In his twenty short years Tim Donovan had been through more perilous adventures than most men experience in a long lifetime. Since the night when, a ragged bootblack shivering in a dark hallway, he had sprung out in time to save Jimmy Christopher from a criminal assassin's bullet, his life and that of America's undercover ace had been linked inseparably. So closely had he followed in Jimmy Christopher's footsteps that he had even attained something of the secret agent's instinctive, sixth-sense feeling for danger....

A dozen watchful guards Tim passed, as he made his way from car to car on his trip to the engine. Then he was climbing into the cab, to watch old Jake Peters lounging at the controls.

Peters' eyes twinkled when he glanced around at the wiry

stripling. "Here he is again," he growled to his fireman. "Come back to pester the life outa me an' try to take over my job!"

With a grin he made way for Tim beside him and soon was explaining the intricacies of valves and gauges that controlled the mighty locomotive.

The premonition of imminent peril faded from Tim's mind and he became just a wide-eyed American youth facing, with itching fingers, a fascinating toy that called to him with every throb of its mighty boiler, every click of its speeding wheels.

"Now, when you're approachin' a blind curve like this ahead," Peters nodded, as the train emerged from the stand of timber that had concealed it for several minutes, "you—"

His voice caught in his throat, clipped short as he dived frantically for the brake. But already the heavy engine was plowing into a mound of piled-up ties and trees heaped on the track to a height of nearly ten feet. With a crash they smashed into the obstruction, grinding through it, slowing down—and then a hail of lead spattered into the cab from every direction. Head and shoulders half out of the window, Peters stiffened suddenly, then slumped lifeless over the sill. At the other side of the cab, the fireman cursed and gasped out his own life in a bloody froth as he toppled to the floor.

As if by magic, masked faces had appeared on all sides— masked faces above blazing guns!

For a split-second Tim gaped at them. Then he was leaning over Peters' dead body, gripping the controls, throwing the roaring engine into reverse. With a mighty clang the train started to move backward—then something seemed to burst within Tim Donovan's skull and blot out everything else....

THUNDEROUS EXPLOSIONS brought Tim back to consciousness. Long moments he lay there in the blood-spattered cab before he realized that the train was not moving—that he had been left for dead with the murdered engine crew. Cautiously, he got to his knees to peer out beyond the tender—just as Captain Howard led that hopeless charge against the grenade-hurlers.

At first Tim did not understand—but when he saw the door of the last freight car disaster in fragments complete realization flashed into his mind. Diane was in that car! They were going to murder her—blow her to pieces with those devilish grenades!

Now Howard was down, his men dropping all around him....

Desperate, Tim spied a horse that was ambling nervously toward the head of the train. Instantly, he was out of the cab, darted toward the animal, taught its bridle and flung himself into the saddle. Slapping his palm against his mount's flank, he headed straight for the knot of murderers. With a shout of rage, he was among them, catapulting into one and grabbing a revolver from the amazed fellow's hand. That gun spat swift death now, as Tim clung to the horse's neck and backed the animal toward the shattered doorway of the car.

"Tim!" He heard Diane's sudden cry behind him.

"Up behind me, Di!" he called, as the terrified animal pranced and reared against the side of the car.

Now she was on the horse's back, arms wrapped around Tim—the animal bolting headlong, snorting with fright as it bulleted its way through. Before the astounded train-robbers knew what had happened their prey had been snatched out of their hands.

Crouched close behind Tim, Diane emptied her revolver at the masked band. Now a score of riders were thundering in pursuit, a fusillade of lead whining after the fugitives. But Tim's double-burdened horse was fast. Urged on by its own terror, it was showing an amazing burst of speed, walking away from the chase—until suddenly it stopped in mid-stride, reared up on its hind legs, then crashed, writhing and screaming in agony, to the ground!

CHAPTER 2
HOODED HEADS

TIM WAS thrown head-first from the saddle, but was back on his feet almost instantly. Springing to the side of the threshing animal, he dragged Diane free from where one leg was partly pinned beneath the horse's bulk. He thrust her down in the shelter of the heavy saddle. But that maneuver was useless. Like a band of rapacious Indians closing in for the kill, the masked riders were circling around them, drawing closer and closer as their bullets embedded in the dying horse's carcass.

Diane's cap had been knocked off in the tumble. Her chestnut

curls fell free around her ears as she raised her head defiantly, determined to meet inevitable death squarely.

It was that circumstance which saved their lives.

"Hold your fire!" a voice suddenly shouted above the roar of shots and thunder of hoofs. "Don't kill that girl! I want them taken alive—both of them!"

"That voice is very familiar," Diane whispered as the dismounted riders closed in warily. "It seems to me I should know him."

The one who had issued the life-saving order was now talking to another masked individual who had ridden up from the train.

Then she was on the horse, her
arms wrapped around Tim!

The new arrival turned quickly to the hemmed-in prisoners, head nodding with unmistakable satisfaction.

"They know who we are," Tim muttered. Hands balled into fists, he tensed, ready to spring.

But Diane's hand was on his arm, holding him back as the raiders overwhelmed them and pinned their arms helplessly at their sides. Into the circle rode the two who appeared to be the leaders. They stared down at the captives with undisguised satisfaction.

"This is even better luck than I anticipated," the familiar voice chuckled. "I hardly expected the train to carry such valuable freight, Miss Elliot. But now that you have come to visit us I shall have to see that you are given every attention Operator 5 would expect!"

With a mocking laugh, he turned to his men and gave orders. Quickly Diane and Tim were tied up, arms lashed behind backs, legs secured to the stirrups and saddles of tethered horses. Helplessly, they waited while the raiders finished their task—the ambushed train being looted of everything the vandals desired. Then the loaded trucks had rumbled off to the south. The outlaw cavalcade reformed and brought up the rear, the prisoners riding side by side in its middle.

Tim's face was grim but his alert eyes watched for the slightest break even in that seemingly impossible situation. Bitterly, he condemned himself for having fallen down on the task Jimmy Christopher had entrusted to him.

Diane's thoughts were centered on that mocking voice, vainly trying to place it in her memory. Then she had it!

"There is a trim little mustache behind that black mask," she said softly to Tim. "I can see it now just as plainly as if he was not hiding his face. That leader is our old friend Doctor Oliver, America's arch-traitor and Number One Fascist!"

"The fellow who used to be president of Stebbins University," Tim added quick identification. "Blaintree's old crony. Jimmy thought he was killed in the Southwest when he tried so hard to break up the wagon train—but devils like this seem to have nine lives."

"Somehow, he escaped the wreckage of Blaintree's rebellion. He was always very good at letting others do the fighting for him," Diane said bitterly. "Now he has a fine outfit of cutthroats of his own—thieves and killers ready to stab their country in the back. That's the answer to these train robberies. But God only knows how thoroughly he has been able to organize, how widespread he has been able to disseminate his traitorous poison. We've got to find that out, Tim, and get news of it back to Jimmy—somehow." Somehow... but how?

NOW THEY were well on their way into the unsettled wilderness. Dr. Oliver's raiders had taken off their masks, and Diane found herself surrounded by hard, criminal faces. Evidently, the renegade college president had succeeded in gathering the lowest elements of Blaintree's old following—scourings of the underworld. Now they were armed with four trainloads of supplies, guns and ammunition that should have gone to bolster the thin line of defense along the Canadian border. Behind the unsuspecting troops in those trenches and fortifications, these traitors were even more dangerous than the raiding hordes that threatened to sweep down from the north! Somehow, those defenders must be warned….

Diane had still found no answer to her problem when the procession reached an elevation from which she could look down into a valley—and observe the first sign of life they had yet encountered. A river ran along the bottom, and five or six miles

RINALDI

down its bank sprawled what looked like a town or an encampment. Smoke spiraled up from it, and the long line of trucks was worming toward it like a magnet.

It was not a town, but the ruins of what had been one. As the rutted road led into it, Diane saw that every building had been pounded to bits by shellfire, gutted by flames. Here her countrymen had once made a desperate stand against the invaders. Now all that remained was the mute evidence of their crumbled homes, their epitaph the stone-lettered "Valley City" still visible above the smoke-blackened doorway of the demolished post office. The new denizens of Valley City had made little attempt to rebuild. Wreckage had been partially cleared from the main street, and a few of the battered buildings had been re-roofed and made fairly habitable, but the main town was now farther down the bank of the Shawnee—wooden huts built in rows like company streets. The place was an encampment for a tatterdemalion army that thronged out to greet the returned raiders and gape at the prisoners. There must have been a thousand well armed renegades ready for any deviltry!

Diane's guards led the way to the one-story ruin of what had been the town jail. A makeshift roof had been slapped over the shell-scarred masonry and a new door had been fitted into place. The interior was still fairly intact—at least so far as the corridor of cells into which she was led. Her captors dumped her onto a hard-mattressed bed, lashing her ankles securely together. Then the door clanged shut, was locked, and she could hear them thrusting Tim into another cell. They leered at her, as they trooped back to the doorway; then the corridor was silent except for the echo of their voices coming from the office just beyond the cells.

Unarmed, locked up here in a cell in the midst of Oliver's stronghold, the situation appeared hopeless—yet Diane Elliot knew that there must be a way out. There *had* to be a way out— and she must be ready for it the moment it arose.

Twisting her bound ankles up behind her back, she groped at the spiral puttees beneath her dungarees, got hold of one end and began to unwind the cloth until her fingers encountered a thin strip of razor-sharp steel. Carefully, she gripped it, worked it loose, jockeying it into position so that she could rub it back and forth against the rope lashed around her wrists.

Tedious, painstaking work—but it had its result. One by one, the strands gave way, until she was able to work the remainder loose, free her hands. Next came her ankles, but now she was careful not to cut the rope too badly. As soon as that rope was

The sharp steel blade bit into his throat!

removed it must go back into place, so carefully arranged as to simulate the actual unbroken binding.

A dozen plans flashed into her mind as she lay there, yet each had its drawbacks. Each was too hazardous, too uncertain to chance recapture and resulting imprisonment from which there might be no hope of escape. There was nothing to do but lie there and wait—listen to the street noises, rumble of voices from the office, the hush that came with night.

Gradually, the dusk deepened; darkness came down. Tensely, Diane waited. Surely they must feed her... and then would be her chance.

But as the long minutes dragged on it seemed that they had forgotten all about her, or intended to let her go hungry. Now only an occasional scraping of feet came from the office. The voices had ceased, the men no doubt gone to their evening meal.

But at last shuffling footsteps grew louder, came down the corridor. A lantern was held up at the door of her cell. The guard peered in, grunted with satisfaction and hung the light from a hook in the wooden ceiling. Unlocking the cell door, he stepped in with a tray of food—and was flung back on his heels as the tray suddenly up-ended and flattened against his face!

Like an uncoiled spring Diane's legs had snapped upward, dashed the tray out of his hands—and then she was up from the cot, on him like a panther, bearing him back against the bars of the cell as the sharp steel blade bit into his throat. "One yell, and I'll slit your throat!" she warned.

But the trembling guard was tongue-tied, mute with terror. He could feel warm blood trickling down his neck and stood like one petrified for fear the blade would sink deeper. Quickly, Diane relieved him of his revolver, motioned him to the cot.

"Lie down," she whispered, and now the revolver muzzle was backing up her orders. "Over on your face."

Meekly, he obeyed and made no attempt to resist as she stripped off his jacket, bound his wrists and ankles, stuffed a gag between his jaws, finally took possession of his keys. Locking the cell door behind her, she hurried down the corridor, located Tim, unlocked his door and, with the bloodied blade, made short work of his bindings.

"Swell, Di!" he chortled, as she thrust the revolver into his hand and led the way back along the corridor. "Now just let me have an interview with Brother Oliver!"

"We ought to get out of this town and send word back to Jimmy without a moment's delay," Diane worried, "but I don't like to go until we know more definitely what they plan. This thing seems to be coming to a head, Tim. They may be all ready to strike. If we only knew where—"

Their decision was made for them when they stepped out of the jail and into the dark street. Hardly had they closed the door and darted into the shadows than a weird, black-robed, hooded individual loomed almost in front of them.

DIANE GRABBED Tim's arm, drew him back into the shelter of a half tumbled-down doorway. Breathlessly, they crouched there until the spectral figure had passed. Then they were trailing it down the street—until another of the same sort appeared. Two more… then a third. There seemed to be a host of them abroad in the ravaged town—a ghostly company that might have been the spirits of Valley City's massacred citizens returning to their ruined homes.

These spooky figures all had the same destination, a two-story structure which had been rebuilt, near the center of town. Diane and Tim crept as close to it as they dared and watched a dozen of the hooded arrivals slip through its dark doorway.

"Looks like a Ku Klux Klan meeting," Tim whispered. "We don't have the password—but we're going to get in there somehow."

They prowled through the rubble, all that remained of the building next to the meeting place. At the rear was an array of broken furniture and packing-cases that must have been tossed from the windows in a vain effort to save them from the flames that gutted the doomed building.

Tim's keen eyes quickly spied a paneless window a dozen feet from the ground at the rear of the rendezvous building. Piling a rickety mound of broken furniture beneath it, he climbed to the ledge and through the empty frame. All was dark and quiet in the closet-like room. Quickly, he reached down for Diane, helped her over the sill.

Cautiously, they opened the door. The cubbyhole into which they had climbed was evidently a committee room toward the rear of one side of a large hall—an auditorium where a mystic lodge appeared to be in session. Nearly fifty of the black-robed, hooded figures were seated in front of a low platform where a speaker was addressing them—Dr. Oliver.

"Today's capture makes our preparations almost complete," he was saying. "All we ask is to keep your men in readiness, waiting for the signal. It should come in less than a month. By then, our European alliance will be complete and our allies ready to step in and help us take over the country. From across the sea, we have the best of news—"

With a half-bow he stepped backward and made way for one of the two black-robes seated on the platform behind him.

"Everything is in readiness," a deep, guttural voice rumbled from beneath the man's poke-tipped hood. "All that remains is the actual signing of the alliance between the three great powers who are backing us. This is a mere formality. Before the ink is dry, loaded transports will be on their way to these shores. Already, our agents are at work recruiting and organizing the men of the Purple Empire who hold Canada. At the signal, this ineffectual Ferrara Line will be overwhelmed, and America will be ours— turned over to you, its regional governors and directors!"

"Three nations!" Diane's whisper was a gasp of dismay, as she crouched behind Tim in the doorway. "America never can withstand such an onslaught! We have all we can do to keep out the invaders from Canada. But now there will be fresh armies, and these traitors from within—"

"The dirty, slinking yellow dogs!" Tim muttered; fingers were tight on the butt of the revolver he gripped in readiness. "Plotting to betray their country to the dictators of Europe! No wonder they hide beneath hoods—they don't even dare face one another!"

"But how about the Federal Government?" One of the hooded audience had risen in his place. "Operator 5 has been sending men into this territory, and we have no idea how much they have discovered."

"Ah, but we have!" Dr. Oliver stepped once more to the front of the platform. "We are keeping very well informed of the activities of Operator 5—from sources closer to him than he suspects. It is not our custom to reveal our identity even to one another at these meetings, but tonight, to reassure you, I shall introduce one of our number—"

He stepped back, grasped the hood of the third man on the platform, tugged it clear, and revealed a massive, leonine head, a deep-furrowed face that glanced around the hall uneasily.

"Governor Robert Emerson!" Oliver proclaimed proudly. "He is keeping us in touch with every effort of the national government!"

"Robert Emerson!" Diane was aghast as she stared unbelievingly into the face of the Governor of North Dakota—the man who had pretended to be so anxious to cooperate with her and Jimmy Christopher in their efforts to run down the train-robbers. "If they have managed to corrupt a governor, Heaven only knows how far they have reached! We *must* get word back to Washington, Tim!"

"And today—" Dr. Oliver's voice rose triumphantly—"we took two prisoners who should bring Operator 5 to terms whenever we are ready for him! But first there are several others who should be 'interviewed'."

Diane had started to draw Tim back from the doorway, intent only on getting out of Valley City. Now she stared as a prisoner was led to the platform.

"Ben Riordan!" whispered unconsciously from her lips.

Only two days ago she had conferred with Riordan in Chicago, had discussed the report he would take back to Jimmy Christopher—now he was a helpless, grim-faced prisoner, arms lashed behind his back, his body covered above the waist only by fragments of his bloody undershirt.

"You were sent to spy on us by Operator 5," Oliver said with deceptive softness as two of his hooded men held the captive. "You were starting back to report to him. Well we are going to save you the journey. You are going to make your report to us—*quickly!* Speak up, man—we're listening."

RIORDAN'S GRAY eyes were narrowed to cold, icy slits in his thin, ashen face; his bloodless lips were tightly clenched.

Mute, defiant, he faced them. He watched the sharp knives bite into his chest and snake a bloody trail down his stomach—watched blazing tapers come toward him and make caverns of hell of the hollows beneath his arms. Perspiration ran down his face and his chest, joined the trickling streams of blood that flowed from his wounds—but not even a groan of agony, came from between his blanched lips.

Tim's finger tightened on the revolver trigger, and the weapon came up to aim—but Diane's hand closed over its barrel. "No, Tim—we mustn't," she whispered a warning. "We *can't!*"

Out there on the platform Ben Riordan had reached the end of his endurance—yet no traitorous word escaped from his lips. He swayed, his head fell forward, and he crumpled in a faint—as brave a soldier as ever charged into a cannon's mouth!

Tim's tense muscles relaxed with relief, and he was aware of the cold perspiration that beaded his own forehead. Softly, he started to back away—only to stop, tense with horror and disbelief. The new captive they were half-dragging, half-carrying to the platform was Captain Howard—the officer who had gone down with his men at the train hold-up!

Howard's face was ghastly—a death's-head rather than a human countenance. Eyes nearly closed, mouth hanging loosely, his head nodded on his chest. His limp legs were unable to hold him up, but two of the hooded devils propped him between them while Oliver shook him mercilessly.

"You were in charge of the troops on that train," the inhuman inquisitor prodded. "You had orders from Operator 5. What *were* they?"

Not a word came from the limp figure. Savagely, Oliver grasped the injured soldier's bandages, tore them away, reopening the ghastly wounds that should long since have caused his death. Only a half-audible moan came from the slack lips, and now the bobbing head sagged all the way over as he lost consciousness or died—Tim could not tell which.

"The fire!" Oliver snarled angrily. "Give it to him—in the face. That will restore him and will loosen his tongue." Fiendishly, they thrust those blazing tapers into the captain's unconscious face—held them there while the horrible odor of burning hair and scorching flesh spread out over the auditorium. Then Tim Donovan's finger constricted on the trigger. That bullet sought the inhuman Dr. Oliver—but at the first report the apostle of Fascism had flung himself flat on the platform, barely in time to save his life. His own automatic whipped out, fired—but fate

27

tricked him. His own bullet landed, mercifully, in the brain of Captain Howard who had fallen in its path.

The hooded renegades were on their feet, charging toward the door from which those shots had come. Tim was already at the window, helping Diane down and climbing out after her. Along the dark street they ran, frantically seeking a way of escape—but now the pursuit was closing in on them from all sides.

Shouts came from every direction. Lanterns and torches began to hem them in—and then Tim spied the gutted shell of a brick building that was still two and a half stories high. Diving into the debris-clogged hallway, he led the way to the second floor.

"Hold them off with the gun, Di!" he panted. "Give me all the time you can—that's our only hope of getting word through."

Then he was clambering up the shattered stairway to the floor above, crouching in the shelter of a half-fallen wall, setting up the compact little magnesium beacon which he had strapped around his body beneath the dungarees.

The effort might be useless, but, scattered through that territory, were other operatives who would be quick to catch such a signal if they were within sight of the flashes—and there was no other chance of speeding the warning words to Washington.

"Tim Donovan reporting from Valley City, North Dakota," he clicked off in Morse code. *"Reporting to Operator 5. Armed rebellion under way in this territory, headed by Doctor Oliver. Watch Governor Emerson—"*

Diane's gun had been barking at the foot of the stairs. Subconsciously, Tim had been counting the shots—and knew now that the gun was empty. Her scream rang in his ears as she tried to block the way with her bare hands, then she was brushed aside. Heavy footsteps pounded up the wreckage-littered stairs, and a dozen figures leaped at Tim, swarmed all over him—to snap off his signaling in mid-message....

CHAPTER 3
GATHERING STORM

"**A**NOTHER TRAIN looted—and the lives of nearly a hundred men sacrificed!" Triumvir Andrew Warren turned haggard eyes from the telegraph message in his hand, and his handsome, distinguished face was grave, lined with worry. "It seems impossible—after all our precautions. Whoever staged this robbery must have known—"

"Exactly," The well-knit, athletic body of the young-looking man in the chair beside his desk leaned forward tensely, the knuckles that clasped the chair arm white with pressure. "They knew. That is why the last three shipments went through safely—waiting for the one we could not afford to lose. Somewhere in our organization there is a leak responsible for the slaughter of those men—and for whatever may have happened to Diane and Tim."

Jimmy Christopher's vital, clean-cut face was stern, alert blue eyes hard, grim. Squarely, they bored into the tired pupils of this man who was the virtual leader and chief executive of the United States of America, even though he shared his responsibility with two others.

After the assassination of President Hank Sheridan, the panic-stricken Continental Congress had decided that the task of directing the destinies of America was too heavy for any one man. From that conviction had sprung the idea of a triumvirate which should divide the work and responsibility between them.

First choice for one of these positions had been Jimmy Christopher, whom a grateful nation had to thank for the overthrow of Frederick Blaintree's brief tyranny—but Jimmy had firmly refused the honor. Public office was not for him while there were so many tasks demanding his attention—tasks which could be handled so much more effectively in the unheralded capacity of Operator 5.

It had been at his suggestion that Andrew Warren, a sturdy New England manufacturer, who had lost three sons and his whole fortune in the struggle against the Purple Empire, was chosen as one of the triumvirs. The other two were General Sylvester Ferrara, whose time was taken up almost completely with military affairs, and Joab Burley, a New York politician who soon developed a penchant for public appearances and little interest in the onerous duties of office.

Uncomplainingly, Andrew Warren had shouldered the huge task of rehabilitating a war-prostrated country, but more and more leaned gratefully upon the dependable judgment and tireless energy of Jimmy Christopher. His eyes softened as he looked at the man who, in less than a year, had become like one of his slain sons to him.

"I forgot, Jimmy," he apologized. "Diane and Tim were on that train. There has been no report from either of them?"

"Not a word—" Jimmy's fingers drummed thoughtfully on top of the desk—"but that is as we planned. If everything goes all right I should hear from them any hour now, but if it doesn't…. Six of my best men have disappeared in that area without sending back a word." He broke off abruptly. "That is more than coincidence. It may mean most anything—at a time when world conditions are as they are today."

Since the disintegration of the Purple Empire, the European and Asiatic nations had resumed their old identities. But, instead of having lost their old feuds and narrow ambitions in the common stress, these seemed to have been augmented by the years during which they were, perforce, laid aside. Now Great Britain and France were frantically striving to rebuild their colonial empires, while the "without" nations were as busily casting about for new fields of their own as they vied for continental mastery.

Germany had emerged from the crumbling empire even more powerful than in the days before the war—this time under the absolute dictatorship of a new *Fuehrer,* Franz Schnabel. To the south, Italy had come forth as a second Roman Empire. Bruno Torbini, its new dictator, had brushed aside the House of Savoy and assumed the title of Bruno Caesar. Between them, these two Fascist autocrats loomed over a war-dazed Europe—and their colony-hungry eyes had now turned speculatively to the New World.

"Marauding bands would not have been sufficiently strong to wipe out all of Howard's men," Jimmy thought aloud; "and they would not have been so thorough in the slaughtering—

31

would not have made it a point to
see that no survivor escaped to tell
the story. This was the work of men
who do not want their identity
known yet—men more anxious to
get hold of guns and ammunition
than food. I have a feeling that I
should be out there, sir—the fate
of the nation may be hanging in
the balance."

"But who will look after your work here?" Andrew Warren
protested in quick alarm. "There is so much for which I depend
on you—that nobody else can do."

His desk telephone interrupted him, and a few moments
later one of the American Intelligence headquarters assistants
stepped into the office with a code message for Operator 5.

"It's a beacon message, picked up last night by R-17, out of
Fargo," he reported. "Came from the west—somewhere in the
center of North Dakota. R-17 signaled for a repeat, but nothing more came."

"—*ting to Operator 5.*" Jimmy Christopher eagerly decoded.
"*Armed rebellion under way in this territory, headed by Doctor
Oliver. Watch Governor Emerson—*" That was all.

"Only a fragment," he almost groaned as he handed the
decoded transcription to Triumvir Warren, "but it comes from
Tim—or Diane. And it confirms our fears. An armed rebellion
with Doctor Oliver at its head—most likely that means Fascist

aid from abroad, a thing we must prevent at any cost. I no longer have a choice, sir—my place is out there in North Dakota."

Andrew Warren's eyes lifted from the portentous message, and he nodded slow, reluctant agreement.

"It would be selfish of me to try to keep you here any longer," he admitted. "The danger is too great. Handle it in any way you see fit. But be careful, Jimmy—America can't afford to lose you now." His handclasp was warm and fervent and the grip of his arm around Jimmy's shoulders spoke volumes. "Good luck to you, boy—and bring back Diane and Tim."

DIANE AND Tim... although he had voiced no word of the fear that gripped his heart, Jimmy fully realized the significance of that clipped-off message and R-17's failure to elicit a repeat. It meant that either Tim or Diane, or both, had fallen into the hands of Dr. Oliver's renegades—or that death had blotted out the warning of the magnesium flare....

In moments like these Jimmy Christopher realized how much Diane Elliot meant to him—what a bleak and unattractive place the world would be for him without her. He realized how fortunate he was in having the love of a woman of such understanding and bravery—who could stifle the call of her own heart when her country needed her.

From the rebuilt Hoover Flying Field, Jimmy caught a transport for Chicago, then a smaller plane to Minneapolis. Nearly seven hours of tedious flying, while he did his best to concentrate on Dr. Oliver and the deviltry he was hatching—yet could not keep his thoughts away from Diane.

Tantalizing questions tortured him until he finished the last leg of the trip by automobile to Fargo, North Dakota's new capital, and located Governor Emerson.

"Watch Governor Emerson," the fragmentary message had warned—but as Jimmy studied the governor's large, craggy-featured face he could detect no signs of guilt. Emerson seemed genuinely worried, harassed by his inability to combat the lawlessness rampant in his territory.

"We have so few people here," he lamented, "and the state is in such terrible shape. Every man is needed at home to carry on the work of resettlement and rebuilding, and the federal troops are all needed on the Line. That leaves these thieves free to work practically unmolested. I thought we had solved the problem with armed guards for the trains. This latest outrage blasts that hope."

"Then you think this is the work of outlaw bands?" Jimmy asked.

"What else could it be?" Emerson glanced up in surprise. "The last troops of the Purple Empire were driven out nearly a year ago, and the Ferrara Line is an effective barrier against raids across the border."

Again, the man's quick surprise seemed genuine—yet Jimmy thought that he detected an uneasiness, a half-veiled fear, lurking beneath it. Perhaps he was wrong, but he decided that it would be just as well not to acquaint the governor with the import of that beacon message—at least not until there had been more opportunity to watch and test him.

"Probably you are right," he agreed with assumed casualness, "but I suspect that the thieves are being tipped off to our plans—

probably by someone on the Line. I want to have a look at the work, anyway—and perhaps we can get a line on the fellow at the same time."

"Very good idea," Emerson nodded promptly, and now there was no mistaking his satisfaction. "I'll arrange it at once."

EARLY THE next morning the governor's car drove them out of Fargo and headed for the Ferrara Line, where Colonel Daniel Porter, who was in command of the North Dakota sector, met them. Porter was about Jimmy's age, well set-up, with a handsome face somewhat marred by a petulant expression around the mouth, a somber brooding in the depths of his dark eyes. He gave the impression of a man on the verge of bursting forth with a protest or a denunciation—but one who had thought better of it and swallowed his rancor.

Jimmy remembered having seen him somewhere. Was it at the Battle of Pittsburgh or at the Continental Divide? He could not remember which—and, oddly, he sensed that Porter understood his uncertainty, and resented it....

Through miles of trenches and underground galleries the colonel led the way, to pillbox machine-gun nests and camouflaged big-gun emplacements. All along the Line they found hair-trigger alertness, bee-hive industry. From isolated sentry posts vigilant eyes were turned constantly toward the north, and behind them men worked like Trojans to complete the construction of the Line that must be made impregnable if America was to be safe.

Jimmy thrilled at what he saw. There was no slacking among those willing workers. Enlisted as soldiers, they were patriots first of all—proving it by the way they pitched into the back-breaking labor. The result was amazing progress in an incredibly short time—but now their zeal was handicapped by lack of adequate supplies.

Many of the underground storerooms were nearly empty. Newly built pillboxes stood ready for the machine-guns which had not arrived, while others were manned by crews who looked dubiously at the scant store of ammunition allotted to them. Even excavations had reached the point where they could go no farther until cement was at hand for concrete.

As he went farther and farther along that great serpentine line of defense, Jimmy Christopher's blue eyes gleamed angrily and his jaw tightened. Now he understood Dr. Oliver's strategy. Not only was he arming his own renegades with the stolen supplies, but with the same blow was crippling the defense so vital to America.

That must be stopped! Oliver must be located, the rebellion nipped in the bud. But how?

Constantly, Jimmy's alert eyes were on the lookout for the slightest suspicious circumstance, for anything that might give him a clue to Oliver's whereabouts or point the way to his confederates—but nowhere could he detect anything.

At last they reached the point where Colonel Porter had to leave them and return to his headquarters. From there Jimmy and Governor Emerson were to motor farther westward until they reached a section of the Line closer to the Montana border.

"There have been some suspicious occurrences in that section." Emerson frowned as he sat back in the car. "Rumors

JIMMY CHRISTOPHER

of insubordination and discontent. It might be that the trouble lies there—if, as you seem to suspect, the raiders are working in conjunction with someone who knows when our supply shipments are to be made. A good part of the last train-load was intended for this section—"

The car had been rolling along a narrow road that clung to the side of a steep hill, halfway to the top. On one side was the precipitous slope, on the other a fifty-foot drop—and the road was in none too good condition. A nasty spot for an accident, Jimmy had made mental note—when at that moment the hill seemed to tremble in the grip of an earthquake!

A terrific explosion roared out above them—and the whole hillside seemed to be in motion, to be rushing down upon them! For a fraction of a second, Jimmy glimpsed the rumbling landslide. Then a huge rock hurtled loose and crashed into the car, to crush it like an egg-shell and brush it off the ledge—down into the yawning canyon!

Over and over the tumbling car turned, while a bedlam of shattering glass and twisting, rending metal filled Jimmy's ears. Grimly, he clung to the back of the front seat while he was pitched from side to side with every lurch and carom. Down, down, like a marble bounced from one to the other of the pins of a bagatelle—and then the car came to a shuddering stop, with a crash that seemed to herald the end of the world....

Dazed, half-conscious, Jimmy slumped in a heap on the overturned car, his legs half out the broken window. Every inch of his body seemed to throb and ache—but now a soothing numbness was stealing over him, dulling the stabbing pain. Vaguely, he could feel something clutching at his throat, choking him—but it was too much effort to try to get loose, too much effort even to cough. The comforting darkness was settling down around him... until something seared into his out-flung hand.

Fire! The warning pierced through the stupor enveloping him—the car was on fire!

Somehow, he got to his knees, reached up to the broken window above him—managed to drag himself up through the frame into the cold air. Fresh breath sobbed into his lungs, and returning strength enabled him to pull himself clear, out of reach of those searing tongues now licking up from the front of the machine.

But Governor Emerson and the chauffeur were still trapped in that blazing wreckage!

JIMMY STAGGERED back to the car and probed inside. The chauffeur was dead, head smashed horribly by the rock that had crashed through the roof. But Emerson was still alive, moaning feebly, gasping for breath.

Tugging desperately, Jimmy tore the jammed door open and got hold of the governor's arms just under the shoulders, dragging him out to a clump of bushes a short distance from the burning machine. Emerson's face was a mass of blood, his skull split wide open. He was barely conscious, scarcely able to open his glazing eyes—and the knowledge of death was upon him.

"… double-crossed me," he gasped, when Jimmy bent over him. "I didn't want any more killing. They were afraid I'd squeal, so they double-crossed me—killed me in the same trap that was meant for you.…"

"They? Who *are* they?" Jimmy pressed, as he bent close to the blood-frothing lips.

"Doctor Oliver… and Richter," came barely audibly. "They are going to take over the government… seize the country. Germany and Italy and Japan will help them… will all attack together… from north and west. Our country won't have a chance…."

His choking voice faded, was drowned out wetly, and Jimmy feared that he was gone. But Emerson clung to life tenaciously. Once more his eyes opened—and now they were clear and rational, bright with that brief moment of understanding that comes just before death.

"When?" Jimmy pleaded. "When, Emerson—when will this happen?"

"Soon… very soon," the dying man murmured. "As soon as they sign… the alliance. Miss Elliot and Tim Donovan—they are in…."

Jimmy clamped his ear close against the faintly whispering lips—but now the last syllable had fluttered from them. Robert Emerson's eyes closed, his head dropped back limply, and he was dead—the revelation he had been about to make forever stilled.

Diane and Tim were alive, Jimmy Christopher decided. They probably were in the hands of Dr. Oliver and this man Richter—whoever he might be—prisoners somewhere in the North Dakota wilderness. Hot blood pounded in his veins and his every impulse urged him to start looking for them, to comb every square foot of the state until he found them—then hang Oliver and all his outfit if either of them had been harmed.

But a warning hand held him back. The voice of duty whispered, stern and uncompromising, in his ear.

Those words from Governor Emerson's dying lips had seared into his brain and clutched at his heart. Germany, Italy and Japan—against such an alliance convalescent America would be powerless. Their fleets would bombard the newly rebuilt ports, their highly mechanized armies ravaging the land from end to end. Such an onslaught would mean the end of the United States—the thorough subjugation of the American people!

But how to stop it?

The one slim hope lay in breaking up that murderous alliance before the agreement was signed, before hostilities actually commenced. Somehow he *must* accomplish that—must turn those ravenous wolves against one another!

Already, swift plans were taking form in Jimmy's brain—plans that must be put into execution at once, without an hour's delay. It might take days, even weeks, to locate Diane and Tim—and every minute of that time America's peril would be increasing, her doom drawing nearer and nearer. He had no right to take that time—no matter how great the danger of his loyal helpers might be. Millions of trusting Americans were depending on Operator 5—and he must not fail them.

Feeling like a deserter, Jimmy crawled along that hillside, keeping to the brush as much as possible so that any of Oliver's spies, who might be watching, would think that their purpose had been accomplished and that he had perished in the blazing car. If they thought him dead, so much the better—that would give an added chance of success to the suicide program shaping up in his brain as he headed back to Washington.

CHAPTER 4
SUICIDE CALL

THE LIGHTS burned late in Triumvir Warren's study the night Jimmy Christopher got back to Washington. Restlessly, the gray-haired old fighter paced the floor, and then came back to where General Ferrara leaned over a map of the Ferrara Line spread on a table before him. He shook his head worriedly.

"Give us two or three more months—and an uninterrupted delivery of supplies and we'll make that line impregnable," Ferrara promised. "But we're not ready now, Andy. Even if all supplies had been delivered on schedule we would have needed more time. Now, handicapped as we are by these shortages, the line is in no condition to withstand the drive of a powerful army. We can keep out the remnants of the Purple armies, but against well equipped legions, fresh from Europe and Asia—well, our men are only human, and you can't hope to match bare hands against lead and steel."

"So our only hope is to wreck the alliance and prevent the combined invasion," Jimmy nodded. "My way is the only way."

"But it will be suicide, Jimmy," Andrew Warren groaned. "Even if you succeed, the chance of your coming back to us is about one in a million. You will die over there—you and every man you take with you."

"But if we *do* succeed, millions of Americans will be saved from death, millions more saved from abject slavery that is even worse than death." There was no show of heroics in Operator

5's words—only the courageous acceptance of the inevitable by a man who had looked death in the face so often that it held no terrors for him. "Those who go with me will not plan to return; any others I cannot use."

"But can't we forestall this alliance in any other way?" Warren was loath to give the consent which he felt would be tantamount to signing Jimmy Christopher's death warrant. "Can't we arrange an international conference—a meeting where we can talk fairly and squarely with representatives of Schnabel and Bruno Caesar—"

"You don't sit down at a conference table with mad dogs, Andy," General Ferrara vetoed. "You don't talk with wolves who are ready to tear you to pieces. I see no hope—unless this plan of Operator 5's works."

The moment Jimmy had arrived with his grave news, Triumvir Warren had summoned his colleague, General Ferrara, apologizing because their associate, Joab Burley, was absent on a "pepping-up tour" of Florida and the Gulf Coast. For hours, the three had talked over every possible way to ward off the fate that hung over the country they served—but at last Andrew Warren was forced to admit that he was stumped.

"I feel as if I am sending you out to a firing squad, Jimmy." His voice shook with emotion. "But I can see no other way of averting this calamity—we are so helpless. God grant that you may succeed and come back to us!"

His eyes were suspiciously moist as he turned away. Jimmy Christopher compared him with the ruthless autocrats who ruled bloodily in Europe, and gave silent thanks that a man of this humane caliber was guiding the destinies of America....

"SALESMEN WANTED—TO introduce American product abroad," ran an inconspicuous ad in the classified columns of the New York newspapers. "Men between the ages of 21 and 30, in perfect health; must speak three or four foreign languages fluently and be perfectly at home in the capitals of Europe. Real opportunity for qualified applicants who are prepared to make a suitable investment." Ordinarily an advertisement of that sort would occasion only a shrug from the experienced job-seeker. Certainly it could not have been expected to attract the steady stream of applicants which flowed into the lower Broadway office of the Acme Exporting Company. Husky young men with broad shoulders and lithe bodies; with square jaws and searching, penetrating eyes. Men of obvious intelligence and capability—and stamped with that something which sets apart those who are able to take care of themselves under any circumstances.

A few of the applicants were turned away by a secretary in the outer office, but most of them proceeded into the inner sanctum—and came face to face with the man they knew as Operator 5.

From New York, Boston, Philadelphia, Baltimore, Washington, Pittsburgh and as far west as Chicago and St. Louis they came; men who had been trained with the G-Men and on the detective staffs of the country's best police forces. Men who had faced death unflinchingly on the battlefield—and who knew that now they might be called upon to face it under far less inspiring conditions. Through the "grapevine" the word had come to them that Operator 5 needed volunteers—and they were on hand.

Most of them Jimmy Christopher knew—men who had served him during the Purple Invasion or men whom he had met in the thick of the fight during those perilous

NAN

years. A few others were strangers, men who came with letters of introduction from reliable agents who could not answer the call in person.

And to all of those who could fill his exacting requirements Jimmy flung down the same challenge.

"America stands on the brink of disaster," he painted the picture quickly, starkly. "We are about to be invaded by an alliance of powerful European nations—about to be invaded and conquered even more thoroughly than when the Purple armies overran our country. Once those invaders reach our shores we are doomed. Our only hope is to prevent that—which is why I sent for you."

He took a breath. "I want volunteers—two hundred men who are willing to follow me to Europe with no thought of ever returning; with the prospect of being shot and buried in a nameless grave in foreign soil. This is a battalion of death I am recruiting—but one that will have no spectacular battlefield finale. The men who go with me must fight alone, must infiltrate themselves into Germany and Italy, must work their way into every possible position from which they can promote discord and arouse suspicion that will cause dissension between these prospective allies. That is our only hope of preventing the signing of the concord which will mean the end of the United States of America.

He faced them, tight-lipped. "To achieve such results you will have to run the greatest of risks—and in many cases it will be necessary for you to engineer situations in which your own death will be an essential part of the *coup*. I am gambling the lives of two hundred Americans against the lives of millions, against the doom of our country—and I am offering you a chance to have a part in that sacrifice!"

Andy Bretton and George Macklin, Sam Baxter and Frank Simms, Tobias Collings and Larry Bridges—those tried and trusted comrades of the invasion days were in the front rank of volunteers.

"Last time, we stopped them when they came over here," Frank Simms said grimly, as memory of his murdered wife and baby flashed into his mind. "This time we'll stop them before they get started—before they have a chance to turn loose their uniformed beasts on our women and children. Tell me what I am to do, Operator 5."

One after another as they filed past him, Jimmy Christopher felt a great warmth welling up in his heart. These were *men*— men who had been tried and found to be true steel, tempered in the blast furnaces of a heartbreaking war. They had earned peace and rest; they had a right to sit back now and let others take their places in the front lines—but they were here, insisting on doing their part, because they were sure they could serve the Stars and Stripes more efficiently than anyone who might substitute for them!

ONE BY one he interviewed and accepted them—to pass them along to the corps of experts who were the personnel of the Acme Exporting Company. Experts in make-up, in disguise, in acting, in foreign languages, in coding and transcription, in all the tricks of espionage; experts in boxing, in wrestling, in swordplay. Men who took those volunteers and worked on them day and night for a week, cramming them through a course of intensive training which must suffice for lack of longer time.

Seven-day espionage graduates who would have to go up against the lifelong-trained master spies of Europe!

Lester Willetts, Charles Whitney, Bub Ellis, Elt Burchell, Tom Ryan—gradually the roster filled up with names that were sufficient guarantee of their owners' integrity. And mixed with them were a few dozen new men, strangers who seemed to have every requirement and demanded an opportunity with the others.

Men like John Mahler, who arrived from Chicago on the third day with a note from Steve Hawkins.

"I can't come myself," Steve had written, "because I am all knotted up with rheumatism—so bad that I can hardly hold this pen. So I am doing the next best thing, sending you a man to take my place. John Mahler is all right, Operator 5—he's the sort you want along."

Jimmy looked up and studied the light-haired, blue-eyed

applicant; a man of about twenty-six or seven, quite evidently of German descent. He could speak German, Italian, French—"and even enough Polish to get by."

"Yes, my grandparents were German-born," he nodded, "but I have had enough of dictators." His eyes narrowed and became as cold as ice. "My father and mother and two sisters—they were all killed when Rudolph's men destroyed our town. I saw those things happen here once—and I don't want to see them happen again. If you need men for work in Europe none can succeed better in Germany than I. I received part of my education in Heidelberg—and when I want to be German, Franz Schnabel couldn't tell me from his own brother!"

Men like that fitted into Jimmy's plans excellently, but there were others where the decision came hard; others whom he had to reject even though he hated to do it. Men who argued and pleaded to be included—who took their rejection as a bitter, crushing blow.

ON THE afternoon of the day after John Mahler had been accepted, Ed Putman was announced. Jimmy Christopher's eyes softened at the memories that name flashed into his mind—and then clouded as he realized the uncomfortable task that now confronted him.

"Sergeant Putnam reporting, sir!" The little man grinned from the doorway—and Jimmy saw that his dark, bird-like eyes were brighter than ever, glowing with the consuming fire of the incurable malady that was wasting his body away. "When do we sail?"

"You don't sail, Ed." Jimmy shook his head in mock rebuke,

tried to make his refusal as gentle as possible. "The men I need must be typical Europeans, men who can lose themselves on the other side and pass for native Germans or Italians—and even a blind man could spot you as a New England Yank no matter how you rigged up. The moment you turned on that nasal twang of yours...." That was as plausible-sounding a reason as any, but Ed Putnam could not be included because he was living on borrowed time—time that might end at any moment his ailing heart was overtaxed. And he knew that as well as Jimmy.

"You're afraid I won't come through." He brushed aside pretense as he dropped into a chair beside Jimmy's desk and leaned forward earnestly. "You think my old ticker will give out on me. But what's the difference, Operator 5? I can't do much battlefield scrapping if we are invaded—but at least I can do my part undercover on the other side. I know what that means— suicide work, probably. And where can you find a man better equipped for that than I am?"

For hours he argued—until the office was closed and the last of Jimmy's assistants had gone home.

"I'd like to, Ed, but I can't," Jimmy finally rose to leave. "Suppose we have dinner together, and perhaps we can figure out some way that you can serve here at home."

Dejectedly, Putnam nodded acquiescence and followed Jimmy into the hallway, waiting while the door was being locked. Downstairs he stood moodily in the street entrance while Jimmy stopped for a paper.

The street was quiet, almost deserted by the home-going throngs, but a taxicab scurried around the corner and drew up expecting as soon as they stepped out onto the sidewalk. Glancing at the headlines of his paper, Jimmy Christopher started toward the waiting machine, was almost up to the half-opened door—when suddenly Ed Putnam flung him to one side, just as a blast of flame and lead belched from the dark interior.

Putnam's revolver was in his hand, was pouring shots into the cab even as that death blast doubled him up and hurled him back.

A split-second more and Operator 5 would have reached out for that door handle—and would have been riddled with lead! Instantly, he understood the trap—and his gun was completing the summary punishment Putnam had started. There were two men in that cab. One lay in a heap on the floor. The other yelled wildly and tried to get out of the far-side door—only to plunge out on his face, the back of his skull a gory, bullet-shattered horror. Terrified, the driver threw the cab into gear as he crouched over the wheel and shot from underneath it—but Jimmy's bullets drilled him through the head.

Leaving the cab to roll crazily across the street and plunge into a store front, Jimmy leaped from the running-board and ran back to where Ed Putnam lay on the sidewalk, feebly attempting to prop himself up on one elbow. Blood was gushing from his mouth, from his riddled chest and stomach—but his glazing eyes gleamed triumphantly and a feeble smile spread over his ashen face.

"It doesn't matter—now," he gasped as Jimmy tried to lift him and make him more comfortable. "I found that way... to serve...."

And Edward Putnam was dead.

A hard lump worked its way up into Jimmy Christopher's throat as he looked down into the sightless eyes of that unsung hero and gently lowered the body to the pavement. Ed Putnam had cheated death; he had died happy in the service he loved—died springing a deadly trap….

Suddenly, Jimmy stiffened—and then he was on his feet, making a bee-line for the building entrance.

It was to avert any possible suspicion, to throw off any of Dr. Oliver's agents who might be stationed in Washington, that he had opened this dummy business office in New York—but they must have trailed him, must have watched the office and timed this trap perfectly. And perhaps that was not all. Perhaps there was another angle besides that waiting cab!

The moment the elevator delivered him at his floor he catfooted down the corridor to the Acme office. It seemed to be dark inside, but he carefully pushed his key into the lock, turned it cautiously, and silently opened the door—to tense the moment his eyes swept the dark office.

There was a light in his private office—the lamp on his desk!

In half a dozen lithe strides, he was at the door, was gripping the knob, turning it—to fling the door open and confront the man who was searching the drawers of his desk! He stared into the open-mouthed, hard-eyed face of John Mahler!

Instantly, Mahler's face twisted into a mask of snarling hate. Like lightning his right hand flashed to a shoulder holster. But before he could drag his weapon clear of the leather Operator 5's bullets were pockmarking his forehead, were slapping him back into the desk chair, the fingers of one hand still gripping the papers he had come there to steal.

John Mahler.... Quickly, Jimmy dispatched a telegram to the chief of the Chicago police, and a few hours later he had the answer—

BODY OF STEVEN HAWKINS FOUND TRUSSED UP IN CLOSET OF HIS APARTMENT. MEDICAL EXAMINER ATTRIBUTES DEATH TO TORTURE.

So that was the explanation of the introductory note John Mahler had presented—a note penned under the duress of insufferable torture, with death to seal the writer's lips the moment his signature was finished! Dr. Oliver, apparently, was not going to make the mistakes of his friend Blaintree; his organization was thorough—and the elimination of Operator 5 seemed to be their first order of business....

JIMMY CHRISTOPHER took extra precautions after that, but there were no further traps or further attempts on his life, and he began to hope that Dr. Oliver's agents had been eliminated. Daily, he worked with his volunteers, instructing them in their duties, outlining the strategy which might help them to insinuate themselves into the places where they would be the most effective.

By twos, threes and fours they booked passage and sailed off for Europe in a steady stream—the cream of American courage and bravery, stealing away quietly to keep a grim rendezvous with death!

Jimmy shook hands with each of them, looked into their

unflinching eyes as they left—and wondered how many of them he would ever meet again. One after the other, until only half a dozen still remained. Two of those had come in to say good-by—but Howard Thorne, the third who should have come in for last-minute instructions, had not appeared.

DAN PORTER

It was not until after the boat on which they were booked had sailed that Jimmy noted the omission. Probably it was nothing; probably something unforeseen had arisen so that Thorne had not had time to come in—and yet the thing plagued Jimmy all afternoon. So much so that he stopped at Thorne's hotel that evening after the office was closed.

Immediately, his half-formed fears became definite when he learned that Thorne had not checked out—but that his room was locked and he did not answer his telephone. Something was wrong! Doubtfully, the hotel manager opened the door with a pass-key—and Operator 5 stepped into the room, to find the first casualty of his suicide battalion.

Howard Thorne lay sprawled on the bed, his head battered in and his throat cut from ear to ear!

Swiftly Jimmy went through the slain man's personal effects, his pockets, his bags—but Thorne's ticket and credentials, everything that he needed to establish his identity, were gone.

His body lay there where he had died—but "Howard Thorne"

undoubtedly had sailed on the *City of Antwerp*, as scheduled; and as Operator 5 stared down at the corpse of the first of his men to make the supreme sacrifice he knew that counter-espionage had been started even before they reached Europe—knew that now they were walking straight into the arms of death!

CHAPTER 5
DEATH'S ROLL-CALL

F IVE O'CLOCK in the heart of Paris. Sit in front of the *Cafe de la Paix* and sooner or later all the world will pass before you, Frenchmen say—and this evening the prediction seemed no boast. It had been raining intermittently and the streets were wet, but the sidewalk in front of the cafe was nearly dry from the steady tread of passing feet. At the tables sat hundreds of men and women, sipping their wine or tea, chatting and waving a greeting to acquaintances.

Toward the rear of the sidewalk enclosure sat an elderly, immaculately dressed man with a close-cropped reddish brown beard and mustache. Idly he seemed to toy with his empty wine glass, but his keen blue eyes were sharp and alert, looking not for chance acquaintances who might drift along in that passing throng—but for *one* man.

"Your Piesporter Doktor, *Monsieur*." The waiter bent over with another glass of wine. "He should be here any moment now—unless something has happened," came softly from his lips as he stacked the "addition" saucer on top of several others. "He knows the importance of being prompt."

"But why didn't he come to the villa?" the bearded man asked, as he lifted the glass to his nostrils and seemed to be commenting on the wine's delicate bouquet. "Surely that would have been simpler."

"He didn't dare—for fear of bringing suspicion down on you." The waiter smiled and nodded pretended agreement. "He is certain that he is being watched and followed wherever he goes—" Suddenly he broke off and his eyes flickered as he glanced out over the light-splashed pavement. "There he comes now," whispered from the corner of his mouth. "From the Place de l'Opera!"

Operator 5 spied his man at the same moment. Picking his way across the street came a well-to-do countryman. His clothing had the unmistakable cut of the provinces, and he glanced uneasily at the unaccustomed traffic that swirled past him.

One moment he was there in the clear, halfway across the street—and then a cab swept out of nowhere, rounded a corner of the Rue des Italiens, and bore straight down upon him. Frantically, the panicky pedestrian tried to back out of the way—but the fender of the taxicab caught him, hurled him backward, directly in the path of an oncoming bus.

A fraction of a second was all that swift tragedy consumed—and yet Jimmy Christopher's unblinking eyes and tense ears missed no detail of it. He saw the deliberate deviltry of that apparent accident, saw how the cab hurtled at its victim. He heard the muffled pop that sounded like a backfire—and caught a glimpse of the dark figure crouched in the cab's window, the flash of an explosion. Then he heard the blood-curdling scream that was wiped out as the heavy bus rumbled over the prostrate man's skull. All in the fraction of a second—and then the cab was gone, swallowed up in traffic.

Sick with horror, Jimmy rose from the table and joined the gathering crowd in the middle of the street. Hard-eyed, he stared down at the still body of the pseudo-countryman—the body of Phil Pendler, who had arranged a rendezvous at the *Cafe de la Paix* because he did not want to risk bringing danger down upon Operator 5. Phil Pendler… another name to be added to the mounting roll of death!

Jimmy stared—and suddenly he was conscious of eyes that were fixed upon him, studying him. Cautiously, he swiveled his gaze, and looked into the waxen-featured, mask-like face of a high-cheek-boned, German-appearing man who stood a few feet from him—looked into deep, unfathomable eyes that were strangely mocking, sardonic. "Very unfortunate," the fellow murmured, "but these inept countrymen are so helpless—so unaccustomed to the dangers of city life."

An ordinary enough remark—and yet it rang in Jimmy's brain with the jarring cadence of a taunting gibe!

IT WAS several hours later when *Monsieur* Henri Boin walked up the pathway to the door of a little villa in the Paris suburb of Neuilly and rang the bell. That tiny blue-and-white villa suited his purpose admirably. It was close to the city and yet sufficiently far out so that its ample grounds screened it from prying neighbors—who otherwise might have noticed and become curious about the number of strange visitors who came to it.

Monsieur Boin waited until the grumbling *concierge* opened the door to admit him, but the moment he was inside the ancient beldame's bent shoulders straightened and her hand came out of the pocket where it had been clutching a leveled automatic.

"We began to worry about you, sir." Arthur Bingham grinned with relief, as he tossed aside the long shawl that concealed nearly all of him but his gray and wrinkled face. "There are ten here so far."

Ten of the two hundred, and a strange company they were—a taxi driver, a bartender, a French army officer and two-Mid-Europeans who claimed to have been officers in the army of Emperor Rudolph, a Russian *emigre,* an Italian exporter, a Czechoslovakian munitions agent, a flower vendor and a public porter. Ten Americans who had "lost" themselves in the bustling, intrigue-seething life of Europe.

Operator 5 greeted them warmly, and took his place at the table at one end of the room. From between the leaves of a dust-covered book, which he carefully plucked from a shelf beside him, he took a sheet of onion-skin paper and spread it on the table. He spread it out and stared down at it with stricken eyes as his soft pencil drew a black line through one of the type-written names listed upon it.

"Phil Pendler—tonight," he said grimly. "They shot him and ran him down in the middle of the Place de l'Opera."

There were two hundred names on that sheet, but since Howard Thorne had led the procession to the grave nearly half of that gallant company had joined him. Some of them had died at sea, mysteriously lost overboard before their vessels reached port. Others had met unusual "accidents" almost as soon as their

feet touched European soil. Some had dropped out of sight entirely. But the rest were burrowing like moles, losing themselves in the new characters they had assumed.

An appalling toll for little more than two weeks activity—

Jimmy sent his body sailing through the air!

and Jimmy knew that the death list must be even greater than he had tabulated.

"Sam Baxter—he is in Munich, playing in an orchestra," he began the dwindling roll-call. "Andy Bretton—he went to Rome as a priest, and there has been no word from him. Harry Craig—"

"He was in Dortmund when the secret police found him," one of the pseudo ex-officers of the Purple Empire reported softly. "They didn't take him alive."

Once more the black pencil smudged its somber epitaph.

"Norman Daley, Luther Davis, Harvey Dexter." One by one Jimmy pronounced the names—and recalled the undaunted faces, the firm handclasps that had been their good-bye.

"Ralph Eaton—"

"Bruno Caesar's agents located him in Modena," the Italian exporter's eyes stared at the carpet as he spoke. "They raided his hotel room and found his German passport and papers, found orders straight from Wilhelmstrasse. They almost caught him when he came back, but he beat them to the munitions works and blew it up before they could follow him inside. All Modena is in an uproar about it, and Schnabel has sent a special emissary to investigate and try to make explanations."

Ralph Eaton's assignment had been one of those in which it had been necessary to "engineer situations in which your own death will be an essential part of the *coup*"—and he had carried out his orders to the letter.

The black smudge which blotted out his name was his accolade....

Fuller, Graham, Haley, Hobbs—the names of men who at that very moment might be facing firing squads or springing the death-trap that would speed them into eternity.

"Henry Miller—he is in jail in Vienna," Jimmy Christopher supplied the details himself.

"He led a raiding party of young Roman Fists into southern Austria and tried to seize the country for Italy. Bruno Caesar has disavowed all responsibility for the invasion—but Schnabel reinforced his army along the Austrian frontier the day after the raid."

Homer Parker, killed in Stuttgart.... David Rawson, died in Trieste.... Myron Thompson, executed in Berlin.... Thad Williams, burned to death in the factory fire he set in Milan.

One by one they joined the company of the dead—with no eulogy but the few soft-spoken words of the comrades who might follow them to the grave at any hour; with no funeral dirge but the paean of sympathy and appreciation which welled up from these loyal hearts that ached for them.

Twenty more names the black pencil had stricken from the roll—and when Jimmy Christopher laid it down he wondered how many more of those who were unaccounted for had already been blotted out of life....

THE JANGLE of the doorbell echoed that dismal roll-call—and instantly Arthur Bingham was darting away into the hallway, clutching the shawl tightly around his head as he hurried to the door. They heard his cracked voice complaining sourly, for the benefit of any possible eavesdropper who might be hidden about the grounds, heard the door close—and then he was back, leading an erect, ramrod figure of a man with unmistakable Teutonic features. A man who wore civilian clothes but had the bearing of a soldier.

William Hubert—Operator 5 glanced down at his roster and congratulated himself that at least that doubtful name could now be definitely placed in the living.

"I haven't much time," Hubert announced as soon as greetings had been concluded. "I had the devil's own time getting away at all—finally managed to wangle a sixteen-hour leave. I am stationed in Frankfort—lieutenant in a regiment that was recruited especially for service in America. There are two divisions outfitting there now—divisions recruited up to full war strength."

"How soon do you embark?" Jimmy Christopher was tense.

"Can't tell about that," Hubert shook his head. "There are plenty of rumors, but nothing very definite—except that there is to be a council of war tomorrow night between the high commands of the German and Italian armies. Supposedly, the last details for the American invasion are to be ironed out—and then we should be on our way."

"How can I get into that conference?" Jimmy demanded.

"Well—" Hubert was doubtful—"I am attached to the staff of Colonel von Koerner. If you could get a German uniform, perhaps I could take you into Frankfort as my orderly."

Operator 5 had already refolded the thin sheet of onion-skin, had put it back in its hiding place, and now he was up from the table, giving crisp orders to Arthur Bingham for maintenance of the villa rendezvous during his absence. Reloading his guns and wadding a fresh supply of currency into his wallet, he was attending to the last few details—when the doorbell began ringing insistently.

Jimmy watched from the end of the hallway, as Arthur Bingham hobbled to the door and opened it on a crack—only to have it pushed back imperiously by a *gendarme.* Half a dozen more surged through the opening, their revolvers covering the *pseudo-concierge* and held warily in front of them as they pressed past him.

Gendarmes—that meant a raid. But why should the Paris police be interested in his activities?

THERE WAS no time to debate that now. Quickly, Jimmy glanced at the windows—and caught a glimpse of a face at one of them, the flicker of light on a revolver barrel. The house was surrounded, and he had no way of telling how many *gendarmes* might be out there on the grounds.

"Your pardon, *Monsieur* Boin—" the lieutenant in charge bowed stiffly from the waist—"but there has been a complaint registered against you. *Monsieur* Richter—" he nodded to a man in civilian attire beside him—"has reason to believe that this villa is being used as a thieves' resort. He has reason to believe that his niece, who entered here last week, has never left the building. It will be my duty to make a search for her—"

"Or for her body," Richter added significantly.

Richter.... That name sounded an alarm in Operator 5's memory—and then he placed it! Richter was the name of Dr. Oliver's confederate—the name Governor Emerson had voiced with his dying breath! Richter—*Monsieur* Richter was his sardonic-eyed, waxen-featured acquaintance from in front of the *Cafe de la Paix!*

"I assure you, gentlemen, there must be some mistake," Jimmy protested—but the *gendarmes* were already ransacking—the house from top to bottom, while Richter stood back and watched with subtle amusement.

"There is nothing in the building," one after another reported. "Nothing in the cellar."

"But how about the grounds?" Richter suggested. "I recall, some years before the war, when a villa like this was used as a robbers' roost and the grounds were converted into a cemetery—"

With lanterns and flashlights, searching parties went over the grounds foot by foot—until they came to a spot which had been recently spaded around a clump of shrubbery. Shovels poked exploringly into the loosely packed earth, turned it aside—and uncovered a man's coat! That set the diggers to work with a will—and soon they lifted from its shallow grave the body of a man whose skull had been beaten to a pulp!

A man Operator 5 quickly recognized as Walter Seeley—one of his own missing agents!

Fifteen minutes later the searchers were digging into another well hidden patch of recently disturbed ground—to uncover the body of Alfred Piquet, the rope which had garroted him to death still tightly embedded in the flesh of his throat. And finally Jeff Carter, his shirt slit to ribbons where traitorous knives had stabbed into his back.

Three more names to be stricken from the roster of the suicide battalion—and now the mute corpses of the victims, buried right there in their own back yard, threatened to climax the defeat of the cause for which they had sacrificed their lives....

Jimmy Christopher glanced up and caught Richter's eyes watching him sardonically, saw the stern-faced *gendarmes* closing in with ready handcuffs—and at that moment he leaped, straight at the too well satisfied Richter. Catching the man by surprise, Jimmy seized his arm, whipped it over one shoulder in a jiu-jitsu grip, and sent his body sailing through the air to catapult into the *gendarme* lieutenant and several of his men and topple them into the grave they had just excavated.

At his first move, the other Americans went into action, and in a moment the quiet grounds had become the scene of a wild mêlée.

"The lights!" Jimmy yelled as his fists lashed into faces and drove into stomachs all around him. "Put them out!"

One after the other the lanterns were trampled underfoot, the flashlights wrested from the *gendarmes* and used as clubs. At one time Jimmy Christopher had been a sparring partner of Gene Tunney's; once he had wrestled to a win over the great Zbysko—and now he needed every bit of his skill to keep those *gendarmes* engaged, to prevent them from using their pistols for a few precious seconds more. An impossible task—but at the moment their bullets began ripping into his little band a sedan came careening from the garage behind the villa. Seven of the Americans were still able to race to the car as Arthur Bingham brought it to a halt and held his hand on the siren, but three of them were cut down before they reached it.

Desperately, Jimmy turned to run back to their aid—but his men seized him bodily and pushed him into the car, held him there helpless until it had sped out of the grounds and roared off into the night.

CHAPTER 6
THEY DIE BUT ONCE

THEY WERE right, Jimmy Christopher admitted as the car passed through the Port de Neuilly and entered Paris proper. For a brief, human half-moment he had forgotten those helpless millions whose happiness and very existence depended on the success of his mission; had forgotten that the fate of individuals must not be permitted to swerve him from his course. While one of that suicide band remained alive, he must go on....

Besides Arthur Bingham, at the wheel of the car, the others who had made the get-away were William Hubert, Anthony Delbar, one of the supposed ex-officers of the Purple Empire, and Tracy Hamilton, who had been cruising the Paris streets as a chauffeur.

"Stop a minute and get out of that female rig," Jimmy again took charge of the situation. "Then we'll drive to Tracy's garage so that he can leave this car there and get his taxi. We're going to the *Cite* Bergere. There's a quiet little hotel there where I have rooms."

Fifteen minutes later Tracy Hamilton's taxi turned into the curious little back alley a block off the Montmartre and drew up at the door of a small, residential hotel. As soon as they were in the suite Jimmy had engaged for emergencies just such as this, he went to work on his face with alcohol, which soon removed the air-brushed beard and mustache. Gradually, *Monsieur* Boin disappeared, and in his place came *Herr* Jacob Meister, a fair-haired man with a duel-scarred face and an abbreviated patch mustache.

From the wardrobe came a change of costume, together with fresh clothing for Hamilton.

"We're going to Frankfort on the midnight train," Jimmy quickly outlined his plan. "Hubert, Delbar, Hamilton and I. You're staying here, Arthur, keeping these rooms—"

Arthur Bingham sputtered a quick protest, but Jimmy cut him short.

"Someone is needed to maintain a contact headquarters here in Paris," he reminded. "Besides, none of us may come back from Frankfort—and the work must go on. In case we fail, it will be up to you to take my place, Arthur."

To take the place of Operator 5! Arthur Bingham's eyes rounded, and his mouth half-opened—but when he shook Jimmy's hand there was grim determination in his proud eyes. He never could fulfill that responsibility, he knew; but, should it become necessary for him to step into Operator 5's shoes, he could at least give a good account of himself before he died in them!

Without interruption Jimmy and his party reached the railroad station and boarded the Frankfort express. Impatiently, they counted the minutes before the train started, but there was no sign of Richter or the Paris *gendarmes*—nothing to give the least suspicion that they had been trailed from Neuilly.

It was a party of four convivial German gentlemen who lolled back in their first-class compartment and hummed snatches of popular songs as the train reached the border and stopped for customs inspection; four gentlemen returning from a gay celebration in the French capital. The customs official grinned at them and gave their bogus passports only a superficial inspection—but Bill Hubert whistled softly and wiped imaginary perspiration from his brow when the compartment door finally closed.

"So far so good," he grinned. "Now if our luck only holds out like this in Frankfort! I'll take you to my apartment and leave you there while I report back to headquarters and see if I can get hold of another uniform," he suggested. "This war council is to be held at seven tonight, in the *Rathaus*. The alliance has not yet having been officially signed, there's been no public announcement of the meeting—but I overheard von Koerner mentioning it over the telephone. The problem will be to get you into the *Rathaus* and then into that meeting, Operator 5."

That *was* a problem, and they discussed it the rest of the night; but when Hubert came back to his apartment the next afternoon with a German sergeant's uniform, Jimmy quickly made his plans.

AT SIX-THIRTY that night they started for the *Rathaus*, Hubert, in his lieutenant's uniform, in front, with Jimmy Christopher, his docile orderly, at his side; and Delbar and Hamilton some distance in the rear. At the door of the *Rathaus* Hubert displayed his credentials to the soldier on guard, was saluted and passed in—but just inside the city hall doorway he suddenly whirled and grabbed Jimmy by the collar while he called to the sentinel to assist him. That was the plan. Surprised, the soldier stepped forward—to be grabbed and hauled inside, where a revolver slapped down across his temple and knocked him out before he had time to utter a sound. Taking his place at the door, Jimmy passed in Tony Delbar and Tracy Hamilton—and held his post there until Delbar, in the sentry's outfit, came out to relieve him.

The first floor of the *Rathaus* was quiet and seemed to be deserted, but there was the sound of voices upstairs. Jimmy and Hubert climbed the broad stairway and quickly spotted another sentinel on guard at a doorway half-way down the wide corridor. He started to salute as Hubert approached—but his hand stopped midway and his face blanched as a revolver muzzle jammed into his stomach. Jimmy's fingers closed around his throat and dragged him into a side corridor where he could be stripped of his uniform, gagged and bound.

With Tracy Hamilton, wearing the second captured uniform, on guard in the sentinel's place, Hubert opened the door carefully. The room beyond seemed unoccupied, evidently an anteroom to the council chamber. He stepped inside, with Jimmy at his heels—and the moment the door closed behind them they were surrounded!

From more than half a dozen points revolvers and automatics were trained on them. As if the click of the closing door had popped them from their hiding places, German soldiers materialized from behind screens, from behind desks and chairs, from closets at both sides of the room—and in their midst was a civilian whom Jimmy recognized all too well.

"Richter!" identification came involuntarily to his lips, and the waxen-featured German grinned.

"Baron Kurt von Richter—of the German Intelligence, as long as introductions are in order," he bowed mockingly, "It is a pleasure to meet you again, *Monsieur* Boin, or *Herr* Meister— or perhaps we had better make it simply Operator 5. Quite a pleasure, considering the trouble to which I was put to make sure that you would accept my invitation'."

Of course, the thing was a trap, Jimmy realized bitterly. They had been under observation ever since they entered Germany, perhaps from the moment they left Paris. This "war council" was a fake—a trap that had been deliberately baited with a telephone call Bill Hubert could not help overhearing. A clever ruse to lure him into Germany in case the attempt to have him arrested for murder in Paris failed….

"Yes, I know you quite well," Richter grinned and chuckled with satisfaction. "It has been very amusing to watch you so amateur American agents trying to play at espionage. I believe there were two hundred of you at the start—and now perhaps fifty are left, no? They, too, shall be taken care of, I assure you— all in good time."

"You may kill us, but there will be two hundred, or two thousand, more to take our places," Jimmy boasted, stalling desperately for time as he tried to figure a way out of that apparently inescapable trap.

Eight guns were covering him and Hubert. Before they could make a hostile move they would be cut down, sieved with lead. More than that, they were standing in the open, out of reach of anything they might have grabbed and hurled or anything behind which they might have thrown themselves. There were two windows—but four watchful soldiers stood in the way of a wild dash and a leap into space....

"No, there will be no more after you." Richter was enjoying himself immensely. "I happen to know that with you, American Intelligence, such as it is, will collapse, Operator 5. But even if more lambs come to the slaughter, they will be too late. By then the concord, which you thought you could prevent, will be signed and our troops will be on their way overseas. Japanese troops to invade your Western states from Canada and Mexico. Italian and German troops to sweep down from the north and split the country down the middle. In a month's time you will be defeated, conquered and subjugated from coast to coast!"

"And while you are doing that, I suppose Great Britain will be standing by and applauding?" Jimmy egged him on.

"Great Britain? Great Britain will be holding every man and every ship at home, lining them up in the English Channel to guard her from the German hosts that will sweep over Holland and Belgium and camp at her very doorstep. Little Britain will have no time for her dear American cousins. No, Operator 5, Great Britain's day is done!"

But even as he lost himself in vainglorious gloating Jimmy noticed that he was watching like a crouched lynx; that the Luger in his hand never swerved. "Now it is to be our day—

the day of the deprived nations who were forgotten when their greedy neighbors carved out colonial empires for themselves. Now it is our turn to take colonies—but we no longer want worthless deserts or malaria-breeding jungles. Great Britain and France can keep Africa and Asia—we will take America and divide it between us. West of the Mississippi has been allotted to Japan, east of the Mississippi and below the Great Lakes to Italy, and Canada will be the German portion. Colonies worth having, those will be!"

UNDOUBTEDLY THE brazen plan Richter was revealing was the truth. Jimmy did not doubt that. Yet he sensed that the man was not telling all the truth, but was holding something back. In the depths of Richter's eyes lurked a suspicion of guile, of trickery....

With one hand he drew a package of cigarettes from his pocket and jiggled one up from the opened corner, grasped it with his lips. Then with mock courtesy he held the package toward the captive he was baiting—and Jimmy's heart leaped. The break had come!

"I prefer my own." Jimmy smiled as artificially as Richter, and his hand started deliberately toward his coat pocket.

"As you wish," the German shrugged. "But remember—the bullets in this gun are dumdum!"

Like a hawk he watched Jimmy's hand come out of the pocket with a silver cigarette-case, watched him raise it and press the release—when suddenly the whole end fell away and a cloud of grayish gas hissed from it!

That much Kurt Richter saw as his finger pressed frantically on the trigger. The figure of Operator 5 melted away before the gun blast—a split-second before it—as he flung himself to the floor. In that same split-second Bill Hubert dived backward toward the door, grabbed the knob and plunged through the doorway just as it started to open.

All of that Richter glimpsed in a panicky flash—and then he was clutching at his throat, fighting desperately for breath as his knees began to buckle beneath him and he felt himself falling.

Kneeling, with his head close to the floor, Jimmy Christopher plucked two objects that looked like thimbles from his vest pocket and stuffed them into his nostrils. Patented chemical filters, they would purify that gas-soaked air for a few minutes—long enough for him to creep to Richter's side and grab his arm, to drag him past the writhing bodies of his helpless men and pull him through the doorway that opened the moment they reached it.

As soon as they were in the corridor, Jimmy drew a flask from his hip pocket and held it to Richter's lips. Its contents spilled into his mouth and gurgled down his convulsing throat. The German wretched, but Jimmy held him tight until the flask was almost empty, then let him sit up on the floor and stare around him—into the muzzle of his own threatening Luger.

"My throat—my stomach—they're on fire!" Richter gasped, as he gaped at his shaking hands. "What did you do to me? What did you give me?" Without waiting for an answer, sudden realization dawned in his eyes. "Poison!" he husked fearfully. "You gave me poison!"

"Right," Jimmy clipped grimly. "Not poison that will kill you

73

quickly—but one that will drag you through hours of agony. By the time your doctors discover what it is and then find an antidote for it you will be past saving. A bullet through the head will be the kindest thing they can do for you then."

Richter's deep-set eyes were wells of abject terror; his wax-like features were as ashen as those of a corpse.

"I know that antidote, Richter," Jimmy told him. "I can give it to you in time to save you—but you've got to move fast. There isn't much time. First of all, we're going out of here—and you're going with us to make sure that we're not stopped. Then you're taking us to the place where this war council is really being held. That's your one chance."

Richter staggered to his feet and almost doubled up as another spasm gripped him. All the bravado gone out of him, he fairly groveled in his desperate fear.

"Anything at all—only stop this burning. It's eating up my insides!" he groaned. "I'll get you out. I'll see that nobody stops you!"

"Remember that your own gun—with the dumdum bullets—will be trained on your spine every moment," Jimmy warned, as they started downstairs and picked up Tony Delbar waiting at the door.

WITH RICHTER in front beside Bill Hubert, Jimmy one pace in the rear, and Hamilton and Delbar, rifles over their shoulders, clicking along behind him, that little procession marched away from the *Rathaus* and through the streets of Frankfort. Several times they met parties of soldiers who saluted and passed on, officers who eyed them indifferently—but nobody attempted to interfere.

It looked as if the luck Hubert had been wishing for was going to hold—when Jimmy's straining ears suddenly caught the sounds of pursuit. He glanced around and caught sight of a squad of soldiers pounding down the street after them, a mounted officer yelling a command for them to halt.

"*Gott im Himmel!*" Richter moaned. "I am powerless. I can do nothing to stop them. If I try to interfere they will think I am working with you!"

"We've got to run for it," Jimmy ordered. "But first give them a volley to slow them up."

Two rifles and two pistols blasted lead back at the oncoming Germans, and then the disguised Americans were racing for all they were worth, following Bill Hubert's lead.

"It isn't far now—not a quarter of a mile," he panted. "I have a car in a garage just outside the Dormstatter Gate. If we can reach that, we'll have a chance."

But now nearly fifty uniformed men were pounding along behind them. Horsemen were spurring in the lead, and Jimmy caught the sputter of a motorcycle. Bullets whistled around them in a veritable hail, and it was only a miracle that kept them from being hit. Twice he halted his flight to pour shots into the pursuers; once to bring down a motorcycle machine-gunner who would have meant their finish had he come a few yards closer.

On and on, racing until their aching lungs threatened to burst—but at last the big arch of the Dormstatter Gate, the old city portal, loomed ahead of them. And at that moment Tony Delbar gasped and went down with a bullet through his groin!

"Leave me!" he begged, as Jimmy and Tracy Hamilton bent over him. "There's nothing you can do for me. I'm finished—but I may be able to slow them up for you before they get me. You can't carry me—"

Frantically, he tried to fight them off, but they wrapped his arms over their shoulders and divided his weight between them. Delbar was a heavy man, and he slowed them up badly. The towering arch seemed miles away, and the yelling troops behind them were cutting down their lead alarmingly. It seemed that they would never reach the gate, much less cover the distance that remained beyond it.

At last they darted beneath it, Jimmy grabbed at one of its pillars for a momentary support—and then Delbar was out of their grip. Wriggling clear of them, he flung himself to the ground and brought his rifle to his shoulder, blazed away at the oncoming men.

"It's no use, Operator 5," he begged. "You can't possibly carry me. You've already taken too much of a chance—if they get you it will be my fault. I don't matter," he fairly sobbed, "but you do! You can't afford to be stopped now—"

"Tony's right," Tracy Hamilton gritted. "He's staying here—and so am I. Between us we can hold this pack off long enough for you to reach the car, Operator 5—but there's no time to stand talking about it."

He hurled Jimmy away from him as he threw himself down beside Delbar and added the bark of his rifle to the other. "Get going!" he flung back savagely over his shoulder. "You have Richter—but he won't do you any good if you stay here and get yourself killed. You've got a job to do. You tend to it—and I'll tend to this one!"

Jimmy Christopher emptied the Luger into the charging soldiers while a myriad of thoughts kaleidoscoped through his teeming brain. Hitherto he had been the one to stand in the gap and send his men on to safety—but now the tables were turned. Now his duty was clear. Tracy Hamilton had pointed the way—and Operator 5 obeyed his orders.

It is doubtful whether they heard his, "So long, men," but they must have felt the eloquent pressure of his hands on their shoulders as he leaped up from his crouch beside them and raced after Bill Hubert and the quaking Richter. Behind them the steady bark of two rifles testified that Tony and Tracy were still alive, still standing in the breach....

And then there came a new sound in the uproar—the heavy boom of more powerful explosions, one after the other.

Jimmy whirled.

He saw that Tracy Hamilton, on his knees, was pulling the pins from hand grenades and flinging them, not at the Germans who were almost upon him—but at the cornerstone of the historic Dormstatter Gate. Terrific explosions sounded—far more thunderous than the report of any hand grenade Jimmy had ever heard.

"My God!" Bill Hubert gasped at his ear. "Those are T.N.T. grenades! Specially prepared for blasting. I had a stock of them in my apartment—and they must have helped themselves!"

T.N.T. grenades—that was it! The old gateway was trembling under the terrific concussions. Pieces of it were falling, raining down on the destroyers—and then a huge section tore loose and thundered down into the road, blocking it completely. It thundered down on two stalwart defenders whose rifles now were stilled forever. Tracy Hamilton and Tony Delbar had attended to their job, and now it was up to Operator 5....

CHAPTER 7
SOLDIER TO SOLDIER

THREE BLOCKS past the Dormstatter Gate, Bill Hubert raced into the garage where he had a powerful supercharged Mercedes-Benz stored. Jimmy Christopher waited with Richter at the door, pushed the fear-ridden German Intelligence man into the back seat and leaped in after him. Then the machine headed out of town before the first pursuers were able to climb over the ruins of the wrecked archway.

"Now, where do we go?" Jimmy shoved the wild-eyed Richter against the side of the car with the Luger muzzle. "Where is that council being held—and you'd better not try any stunts if you expect to live to see the sunrise!"

"*München!*" Richter quavered. "In Munich—in Crown Prince Rupprecht's former castle. But we can't wait that long—it will take four or five hours. There will be nothing left of my stomach by then! It's in Munich, I swear it—" Jimmy eyed him searchingly and decided that the fellow was telling the truth—or at least part of the truth. When they reached Munich another trap might be waiting for them, but at least that city probably was the meeting place where the final preparations for the American invasion were being discussed.

"You will keep for a while," he tersely dismissed Richter's babbling pleas. Then his thoughts turned to the situation ahead, began fabricating plans that must be put into execution as soon as they reached the Bavarian capital.

The Mercedes-Benz would do a hundred and twenty miles an hour, but the winding road seldom permitted an approximation of that speed. One after the other they sped through sleepy German villages like an express train whisking past a flag-stop. On and on into the night—but now Jimmy began to watch Kurt Richter curiously.

The German's moaning had ceased and he was beginning to stir restlessly, his eyes darting from Jimmy to Bill Hubert speculatively. In those eyes suspicion was beginning to dawn.

An hour and a half out of Frankfort realization broke over him.

"You tricked me!" he snarled. "You lied to me!" his voice rose to a harsh yell to make himself heard above the droning purr of the super-charger. "That was no poison you gave me!"

"Your belly's beginning to feel all right, eh?" Jimmy grinned. "I figured you'd wake up about now. All you swallowed was concentrated essence of peppermint with a bit of burnt-almond flavoring to make you certain that it was cyanide. No, you're not poisoned, Richter—but there is still plenty of lead poisoning in this gun. Just to be sure that you don't try anything foolish, it might be better to tie you up," he decided. "Take off your belt."

Richter fumed and spat curses, but did as he was told. Help-lessly, he sat there while his arms were strapped to his sides. Then at last he could master his rage no longer.

"Yes, the council city is *München,*" he snarled vindictively, "but I didn't tell you that the meeting was held this evening! It is all over by now, and there will be nothing you can do when you get there. The *generalissimo* will have gone back to Italy, and the plans for overrunning your America will be under way!" He leered.

That was the ace Richter had held up his sleeve, Jimmy realized bitterly—that was the treachery he had sensed in the fellow's manner. By the time they reached Munich their trip would be for nothing. Yet now there was nothing to do but go on with it.

"We'll cross that bridge when we come to it," Jimmy snapped, with a show of confidence he was far from feeling.

As the miles sped past, his thoughts kept pace with the roar-ing engine, feverishly formulating fresh plans and seeking a solution for this new development. First of all, there was the problem of what to do with Kurt Richter. A forest on the edge of Munich provided the answer.

Hubert drew up beside the road and helped Jimmy tie the German's ankles securely with strips ripped from his own shirt. Gagged and trussed up so that he could not possibly free himself, they lifted him between them and carried him three or four hundred yards into the shelter of the park-like woods. There he should be safe for some hours and yet be certain of eventual discovery by a touring forester.

Helpless, Richter snarled up at them and his eyes glared murderous hate—a grim promise that the score was not settled—as they left him.

THE SKY was gray with dawn when Hubert parked the car well inside the city. From there Jimmy led the way on foot, alertly watching for any evidence of the Italian visitors. But there was none. As Munich came awake it went about its business as usual, with no apparent indication that a momentous war council had just been held there—until they mingled with a crowd that thronged the square in front of the *Feldherrnhalle.*

The great outdoor bandstand was aflame with German flags, but mingled with them was the red, white and green standard of Italy—and the German military band, giving a concert, was rendering the Italian national hymn!

Jimmy glanced around him and could see little enthusiasm except among the younger element of the crowd. Then his eyes met those of his neighbor, a stalwart Bavarian countryman of about fifty.

"Now we should take off the hats and cheer for that flag," the old man muttered, "but I remember when it brought death to my two brothers. I remember when we fought against it on the Austrian frontier. But these *dummkopfs*—they forget the betrayal of 1916! They forget how these same Italians stabbed us in the back!"

His eyes were bleak with bitter memories. As Jimmy Christopher stared into them he recalled that Franz Schnabel, the former stonemason who was now Germany's dictator, had also fought and seen his comrades shot down beside him on the Austro-Italian frontier....

"Some of them forget—but not all of us, my friend," a voice on the other side of the countryman rumbled softly. "Watch the towers of the *Frauenkirche* at noon, and you will see something that should not displease you too greatly."

That voice tingled familiarly in Jimmy's ears. Quickly, he changed his position, backed through the crowd until he could see the speaker's face—and then his swift suspicion was confirmed. That seeming cynical-eyed German was Fred Insley—one of his own men!

Now Insley was easing his way through the crowd, edging up to another glum-faced oldster to whet the old fellow's disapproval.

But what had he meant about the *Frauenkirche* at noon? Jimmy glanced at his watch and saw that it was nearly eleven-thirty. As quickly as possible he wormed his way after Insley, caught up with him and tugged at his arm. Their eyes met—and Insley blinked understanding.

A few minutes later he had backed out of the throng and joined Jimmy at its edge.

"What is this about the *Frauenkirche?*" Operator 5 asked at once.

"The best possible *coup!*" Insley exulted. "We have Marshal Rinaldi, the *generalissimo!* Sam Baxter planned it. There are six of us here in town—Mousley, Herndon, Baker and Ellis, besides Sam and me. Last night, after the German-Italian war council was over, Rinaldi and his staff—there were four of

82

them—started to drive back to Italy. But we overhauled them and pushed their car off the road. We had them disarmed before they knew what had happened to them."

He went on. "Sam has a private garage rented down in Starnberg, where he kept the car—so we ran the Italians' car in there, instead. We tied up the staff men so tight that they won't be able to get loose for a week. Gave them all a hypo, to make sure that they don't come to for at least twenty-four hours, and then we left them locked in the car. All except Rinaldi—we've got him right here in town!"

His eyes gleamed. "Early this morning, after we got back, we broke into the *Frauenkirche* and overpowered the sexton—put him to sleep with a hypo. We took Rinaldi up into the south tower, and he's there now. Baxter and Mousley and Ellis are with him, while the rest of us are drumming up an audience who ought to appreciate the performance. *At noon we're going to hoist him out of the window and hang him!*"

Jimmy Christopher gasped as he visualized that scene—the streets around the great church that dominates all Munich crowded with curious Germans; and then, swinging out over their heads from a window high in one of the Byzantine domed towers, the lifeless body of the marshal who was to have commanded the invasion of America!

"We've made all our plans so that the hanging will be blamed on the Germans—made the staff officers think we were German secret police," Insley grinned. "If that doesn't split this alliance wide open, nothing ever will! Bruno Caesar ought to be declaring war on his intended allies by tomorrow morning, and old

Schnabel will have his hands full without sending a man to America!"

It *was* a brilliant *coup*, one that was staggering in its audacity. But Operator 5's human heart, his sense of fair play, revolted against the cold-blooded hanging of a man who had not yet lifted a finger against America—a soldier who, if he planned and headed the proposed invasion, would only be doing his duty to his own country. That was the sort of strategy Franz Schnabel or Bruno Caesar would have applauded—but it was not the American way.

"It won't do, Fred," he vetoed regretfully. "That's too much like cold-blooded murder, even for a cause as vital as ours. But—" as he saw Insley's face cloud with disappointment—"you've done a mighty fine piece of work in snagging Rinaldi. I want to have a talk with him—and before I am finished I think we may still save America."

A near-by clock chimed the quarter hour—a quarter to twelve—and Jimmy realized that there was no time to spare. It would take all of ten minutes to reach the *Frauenkirche*, and then climb up into the lofty tower....

A CROWD had already gathered on the sidewalks across the way from the cathedral when Jimmy and Insley hurried toward the wide doorway. Heads were craning upward, eyes turned toward the towers curiously, as the noon hour drew perilously close. Husbanding his breath as best he could, Jimmy raced up flight after flight of the steep, winding stairs, panted his way to the door of the tower room—and was almost flung back headlong when Bub Ellis sprang from concealment and lashed out at him with a gun barrel.

"Operator 5!" he gasped amazed recognition just in time. Then Jimmy was past him, striding into the little cell-like room where Marshal Vittorio Rinaldi sat, bound hand and foot, before the open window through which he was to be hoisted.

A long rope was knotted in a loop around the doomed man's neck, its other end secured to a heavy table in the cubicle. Over him stood Sam Baxter, watch in hand, counting the minutes before Rinaldi would be hurled out over the ledge to his death. Grim-faced and tight-lipped, the soldier sat staring out over the far-stretching panorama of house-tops—and then came his unexpected reprieve.

"All right, Sam." Operator 5 held up his hand, as his men turned astonished eyes toward the doorway. "Let me have a few words with the marshal before you proceed."

Obediently, Sam Baxter dropped the rope and stepped back, while Jimmy strode over to Rinaldi and cut the thongs from his wrists and ankles.

"You are in the hands of the American Intelligence, Marshal," he addressed the wide-eyed officer in his native Italian.

The old warrior bowed courteously. "In the hands of Operator 5—the man who caused Emperor Rudolph so much trouble," he corrected. "I heard—from the doorway."

"We do not want to hang you, unless you force us to do it," Jimmy assured him earnestly. "It will be much more satisfactory if you will listen to reason. I understand that you have completed your plans for the conquest of America and have agreed on how our territory is to be divided with your allies. Now I want you to give up those plans, for the sake of your country as well as mine."

Jimmy frowned. "You think it is America that Franz Schnabel plans to conquer—but his eyes are really on your own Italy. Don't you realize that there is not enough room in Europe for two empires such as Schnabel and Bruno Caesar are building? Don't you realize that one or the other will have to dominate—will have to gain undisputed mastery of the continent?" He let that sink in.

"This invasion of America—the brunt of it will be borne by Italian troops, will it not?" Jimmy hazarded, gambling on the fact that Rinaldi was to be the supreme commander—and in the momentary flicker of the marshal's eyes he saw that he had guessed right. "Italian troops which will be drawn far away from Europe," he pressed. "Don't you realize how that will weaken your defenses at home—how wide open it will leave Italy to invasion? While the Roman legions are far across the seas, Franz Schnabel will dictate his own terms—or his armies will march from one end of Italy to the other!"

Vittorio Rinaldi's olive-hued face was pale. His short-clipped gray mustache twitched nervously, and uncertainty was plain in his eyes. For a moment, he seemed to hesitate—and then his hands were thrust out eloquently, palms upturned.

"Claims—nothing but unsupported claims, *signor.*" He shook his head. "You say that Franz Schnabel will break faith, that he will betray us, but you have no proof—nothing but your word."

"Nothing but that—and Schnabel's record," Operator 5 reminded. "He has kept no agreements—broken his word

86

whenever it served his purpose to do so. He had little use for Italy until he conceived the idea of this American invasion—as bait to weaken your nation so that his mastery will be unquestioned. I need no better proof!"

But Rinaldi was shaking his head firmly, and now the momentary doubt had gone out of his eyes; his decision was made. Helpless prisoner that he was, he could not be persuaded to bargain for his life.

"Only your unsupported claims," he insisted. "I cannot alter my plans—and if you kill me another *generalissimo* will be appointed to take my place. But—" he eyed Jimmy squarely—"bring me proof of what you say, and that will be another matter. Then my hands will certainly be freed."

"Your word on that, Marshal?" Jimmy Christopher held out his hand—and Vittorio Rinaldi clasped it.

"The word of one soldier to another." He smiled. "Bring me proof of what you claim and I will terminate the American campaign!"

CHAPTER 8
WOLF AND EAGLE

RINALDI'S OFFER was plain and unequivocal: bring him proof of Franz Schnabel's duplicity and he would withdraw from the invasion of America. That put the responsibility squarely up to Operator 5—as seemingly impossible an assignment as any secret-service agent ever undertook!

To pry into the secrets of the most powerful and well

guarded chancellery in Europe and secure positive proof of their double-dealing, and that within a matter of days, or even hours....

Where should he begin?

Jimmy Christopher pondered that question as he stood at the little side door of the cathedral and waited until Sam Baxter arrived with a car; as Insley, Mousley and Ellis came down with the marshal and smuggled him into the rear of the machine before curious eyes could identify him. All the way to Starnberg, he debated his problem—and by the time they reached the garage where the Italian car with its slumbering staff officers was stored he had a lead... had begun to formulate a daring plan!

Kurt Richter—there was the answer. The German agent would know what his general staff was planning, and he would talk. Jimmy was always reluctant to resort to torture to loosen a man's tongue, but, judging by the yellow streak Richter had exhibited, that would not be necessary—threats and preparation would be sufficient.

Richter would talk, and if the information he divulged was not sufficient Operator 5 would get more—as Richter himself! Once in possession of the German's papers and clothing, his face made up to counterpart Richter's wax-like features, Jimmy would go right to Berlin—make a desperate bid to reach Franz Schnabel and force a confession from him! A mad scheme—yet nothing but a daringly mad scheme could save America in this crucial hour....

Back to the forest on the outskirts of Munich, Sam Baxter drove, to draw up cautiously, as Jimmy directed, a short distance from where the Mercedes-Benz had stopped to dispose of Richter. The road was deserted, and the place looked just as it had in the early morning hours—but Jimmy was taking no chances.

"You stay here at the wheel, Sam," he directed. "The rest of us will go in for him. Spread out around me, close enough so that you can keep in touch with one another—and keep your eyes open."

The forest was silent, except for the soft murmur of the light breeze sighing through the pines. Underfoot, kept as cleared and well trimmed as a park lawn, there was no brush to snap beneath their feet, not a sound—until suddenly the stillness was broken by the cough of a muffled automatic, and Fred Insley clutched wildly at a tree trunk as he tottered and fell on his face!

Instantly Jimmy Christopher was at his side, staring down at the ghastly hole a dumdum bullet had ripped through the back of his skull—and then the quiet forest aisles seemed alive with men. Shots came from all sides, bullets whistled through the air and thudded into tree trunks—and now the muffled reports were being echoed by the louder bark of answering guns as Jimmy's men went into action.

But they were outnumbered, trapped—and might be surrounded!

"Back to the car!" he shouted, as he started to edge his way toward the road. At that moment he spied the man who had killed Insley.

Jimmy stepped out to face him—and brought the fellow down with two deliberate bullets. Then he was beside him, grabbing the inert body and lifting it over his shoulders. Staggering under the weight, he pounded toward the waiting car, until Bub Ellis sprang to share the burden. Between them they thrust the groaning prisoner into the machine.

"They got Mousley," Ellis gritted, as he blasted a shot back at the Germans who were sniping at them from behind the trees— and then the car was underway, was out onto the road as a hail of bullets shattered the windows and bored into the side and rear.

"Straight ahead—just keep going," Jimmy clipped directions as he turned to his captive.

The fellow was close to death, but he was still breathing feebly. His terrified eyes were open and his trembling lips were drooling almost inaudible sounds that might have been words. Jimmy propped him upright and tried to staunch the blood that spurted from his chest wounds, made him as comfortable as possible. The dying man's eyes mirrored his thanks—and Jimmy took quick advantage of it.

"You are of the secret police," he said close to the fellow's ear. "You know what is planned for this American invasion. You know what Schnabel intends for Italy—"

But the German shook his head feebly.

"I know very little… nothing," he whispered. "I do only what is directed. The chief… he knows why things are done."

"The 'chief?'" Jimmy pressed. "The chief?"

"Kurt von Richter… the chief… of the secret police," came in a blood-flecked gasp; and the man was dead.

Kurt von Richter, chief of the German secret police! Operator 5 had held him prisoner—but let him slip through his fingers! Bitterly, he upbraided himself for his carelessness, realizing that the task ahead of him was now doubly difficult. He and his men were recognized and known, and now every secret agent in Germany would be grimly searching for them!

Now the soldier's uniform he wore would be useless—would only serve as a magnet to draw attention to him. Quickly, Jimmy stripped it off and put on the suit he took from the dead German's body. It was a temptation to use the man's papers, but that would be too dangerous—too sure a way to be trapped the moment they were reported to the police.

Jimmy pocketed them and carefully rolled up the uniform. Both might serve him at some other time. Carefully, he worked on his face with his make-up kit. When he was finished, *Herr* Otto Piening could easily be identified from the photo on the passport he selected from several that were strapped tight to his body in a thin, silken, corset-like vest.

"I am leaving you at Augsburg," he told the others, when they had hidden the German's body behind a clump of bushes near the road. "After this it must be every man for himself. We have all been seen, and each will add to the danger of the others if we are together. Separate as soon as you are out of Augsburg, but keep in touch with me there—and remember, proof of Franz Schnabel's real plans is the only hope for America!"

AT A quiet, side-street *pension Herr* Otto Piening left them. There he engaged a large, ground-floor room with windows close to the street level, and there he maintained his headquarters for six long, nerve-wracking days while he exhausted every means of locating Richter. The secret-service chief seemed to have disappeared—but his agents were untiring.

Day by day, news of their activity filtered back to Operator 5. Day by day, the black pencil traveled across the flimsy sheet of onion-skin, and the roll of the dead grew longer. And with each passing hour the doom that hung over America drew nearer and nearer.

Now Jimmy was cut off from all word from home. He had no way of knowing what progress Dr. Oliver's renegade organization was making or what had become of Diane and Tim Donovan. It was more than six weeks since he had heard from them—more than six weeks since that fragmentary beacon message had come out of the North Dakota wasteland that had swallowed them up....

Half a dozen times Jimmy had been certain that he was watched, trailed; but the watchers never closed in on him. It was as if they were content to keep him under surveillance—and to strip his men from him one after the other. Desperately, he tried to break through that invisible cordon—to bait traps for Richter's agents, gambling on the chance of capturing one of them and forcing him to lead the way back to his chief. But they ignored him—until the evening of the sixth day.

Standing outside the windows of the Augsburg *Bulletin*, Operator 5 had felt the chill fingers of defeat clutching at his heart as his eyes stared up at the latest news flashes.

"Reichsfuehrer Schnabel to Confer with Bruno Caesar!" the dispatch screamed at him—and he knew that the hour he had been dreading was close at hand. That meeting was to be on the next day, in Vienna, now the capital of the German province of Austria. In that historic city, the scene of so much diplomatic

skullduggery and so many secret conferences, the Fascist dictators of Europe would meet to sign the concord that would seal the fate of the United States of America!

But that compact must never be signed! In some way the conference must be disrupted, the signing prevented—and now the only place in which that might be accomplished was Vienna!

Quickly, Jimmy Christopher started back to his *pension*, while his brain seethed with desperate plans. He must get to Vienna without delay, see to it that Bruno Caesar met a reception there such as he little expected—a reception that would terminate this threatening German-Italian alliance for all time. First, he would have to return to his room to meet Sam Baxter, who was to be there at six.

But as he strode along the quiet street toward the *pension* a sudden warning rang in his brain. There was something wrong, something unusual about the familiar street… and then he knew what it was. The sound of his footsteps seemed too loud—like those of a man walking through an empty hall, or through a room that was crowded with breathlessly silent watchers. The street was *too* quiet tonight!

Clop-clop, clop-clop—the sound of his steps reverberated in a stillness that would have echoed with the fall of a pin. Now Jimmy could fairly feel the watching eyes boring into him. But there was not a soul on the block, not a person in sight as he came within a hundred feet of the *pension* doorway—just as an automobile drew up at the curb.

It was the Mercedes-Benz, Jimmy recognized. Bub Ellis was getting out, starting across the sidewalk; Bill Hubert had his foot on the running-board—and at that moment a thunderous bedlam broke loose! Instantly, the large center window of Jimmy's room crashed out into the street—and through the shattering glass hurtled Sam Baxter! His arms tied behind his back, he dived headlong—but even before his body hit the sidewalk it was riddled with bullets!

Shots blasted at him from the room he had just quit, from the doorway of the house, from buildings across the street. It was a fusillade of lead that poured into Ellis from two sides, spun him around and toppled him to the sidewalk before he could draw his gun.

In a fraction of a second Jimmy Christopher glimpsed Sam Baxter's bloody face, his mouth gagged so that he could not shout an alarm. He saw the incredulous amazement on Bub Ellis' features as leaden death lanced through him. Then his own weapon was in his hand, roaring and kicking as he ran forward in a crouch, firing at a dozen men who had suddenly materialized out of nowhere.

Instantly, he realized what had happened—understood the trap which had almost claimed him. Deeming it better to eliminate him before he could make any attempt to interfere with the Vienna love-feast of the dictators, Kurt von Richter had given the signal to draw in the net. Taking possession of Jimmy's room, the secret police agents had been waiting there for him… when Sam Baxter, arriving ahead of time, had stepped into the trap.

Bound and gagged, Sam must have seemed utterly helpless as he was forced to sit and wait for his chief to walk, unsuspecting, to his doom. But the German agents had reckoned without that disdainful disregard for death which had become so prevalent among American patriots during the terrible years of the Purple Invasion. They had reckoned without that tremendous personal loyalty which would have prompted any of Operator 5's men to lay down his life cheerfully for the man upon whom America's fate rested.

Sam Baxter, the survivor of many a bloody battlefield, had heard the final summons in a quiet street of a sleepy German town—and had answered it without flinching!

Those things flashed through Jimmy Christopher's mind in a surge of understanding as his finger instinctively triggered his weapon. Baxter was dead, Ellis was dead, Hubert was swaying there at the door of the car, and the Germans seemed to be closing in in droves. This was the end, Jimmy knew—the end for him and for the mission on which Triumvir Warren and those other trusting friends were depending so hopefully....

The end came in a fearful stab of pain that seemed to split his head wide open—in a burst of blinding white light that engulfed him as he felt his knees buckling beneath him, felt himself falling....

It was the rush of cool air that brought him back to consciousness and a world of roaring noise and throbbing pain. That noise.... At first he could not place it, then gradually he realized it was the purring of the super-charger of the Mercedes-Benz. That ghastly pain... was his head, throbbing as if a great drum were being pounded inside his skull. He reached up and felt a bandage around his head, saw Bill Hubert, at the wheel, looking at him.

"Take it easy," Hubert advised. "You probably feel like hell, but you'll be all right in a little while—you were only creased. A fraction of an inch more and your skull would have been trephined from front to back. As it is, you only lost a bit of hair and scalp."

"How did I get here?" Jimmy asked groggily. "I was falling—"

"And I grabbed you," Hubert finished.

"You grabbed me, got me into the car—and drove out of that death-trap," Jimmy said slowly. "Thanks, old man." Then, as he peered out at the rural landscape that was barely visible in the deepening dusk, "Where are we headed?"

"Vienna," Hubert told him. "I thought that was what you'd want."

And Operator 5 sank back against the seat with a sigh of satisfaction—with the surge of heart-warming appreciation that sometimes comes to a man who knows that he is served by loyal friends who are efficiently capable and utterly dependable... friends who can be relied upon while a drop of blood flows in their bodies!

VIENNA WAS fairly buried under flags and bunting. On every light-post the crimson, swastika-emblazoned banner of Germany was entwined with the red, white and green of Italy. From every house-front yards of crimson drapery gave the streets the appearance of canyons bathed in blood. And on the sidewalks, in front of those red-walled buildings, were jammed thousands of spectators, held back by rows of steel-helmeted troopers.

Bruno Caesar was coming!

THE SUICIDE BATTALION

A murmur of excitement ran along the close-packed Ringstrasse as they caught the first strains of martial music—and then a proud German army band came goose-stepping into view. After them marched the impressive, shiny breast-plated and Roman-helmeted ranks of the Italian dictator's bodyguard; followed by Bruno Caesar's car—on its way to the momentous conference with Franz Schnabel in the great halls of the *Neue Burg*.

"*Heil*, Caesar!" the crowd thundered, and the German troops came to smart attention.

Hysterical bedlam kept pace with that slow-moving car—but, suddenly, above the roar of the crowd, rang out a new note that was unmistakable, that threw the procession into wild panic. The sound of shots—fired at Bruno Caesar!

Frantically, the dictator's bodyguard rushed to his open automobile, cloaked it with their bodies as leaden slugs shattered the windshield and spanged off the hood. The shots came from somewhere aloft—from the top floor of one of the Ringstrasse buildings. Open-mouthed, the crowd gaped up at the open window, and for a fraction of a second a hushed silence gripped them. Helpless, fascinated, they stood there and watched that crouching figure—beheld the pointing muzzle of the automatic blast flame as Bruno Caesar threw himself flat on the floor of the car and a bullet ricocheted off the mudguard.

Twice more that automatic spoke—and then the man dived back into the apartment behind him, as a score of policemen and soldiers stormed through the entrance of the building.

Operator 5 had been sorely tempted as his finger pressed the trigger of that deliberately pointing Luger—beside himself to send a bullet crashing into the brain of that swaggering tyrant. But that would do little good; it would simply mean that another dictator would arise to take Bruno Caesar's place. It was much better to have the man alive—cowering in abject terror and then flaming into savage anger at memory of his narrow escape from death.

Death was the only thing Bruno Caesar understood—death and treachery. Operator 5 planned to give him a sample of both.

"They're coming!" Bill Hubert called from the hall doorway. "Not much more time. They're through the entrance—coming up the stairs!"

Calmly, Jimmy Christopher pressed the trigger for his last shot—and buried a bullet in the leather cushion of the seat from which Bruno Caesar had flung himself! Apparently incensed at his miss, he stood up in full view at the window and shook his fist at the cowering autocrat—stood up so that those raging Italian eyes could not miss his German lieutenant's uniform, the Teutonic mold of his features….

Then he was leaping back into the room, dropping the empty Luger beside the front window, racing into the hall and back to a dormer window at the rear of the building. Down that sharply sloping roof he went to a ledge that ran along its edge. Close at his heels came Bill Hubert, clinging precariously to the ornate cornice as they crawled along the house next door. There a thin steel folding extension ladder awaited them, and they lowered themselves to the roof of the building next in line.

One building more, and the far end of that roof—the extension ladder would be raised again. Then they would climb through another dormer window and into an apartment where a complete change of clothing awaited them—new identities. They would quickly change places with the two lifelike dummies that were propped up in the front window, gazing out at the procession. A perfect alibi, if one should be needed.

The carefully devised plan had worked without a hitch. The tenants of that first apartment, left tied up helplessly on the floor, would tell an excited story about two German officers who had knocked on their door and overcome them before they could even think of resisting. They would tell of lying there and watching the assassins wait for Bruno Caesar's car to arrive—would testify to hearing them talk as if they were obeying orders from Kurt von Richter!

Everything had worked to perfection, and now the chances were hundred to one that Bruno Caesar, shaken by his close call, would fly into an unreasonable temper. In the light of that testimony, he would see nothing but rank treachery—would accept no other explanation. It would disrupt the scheduled concord-signing—putting an end to Franz Schnabel's scheme for a raid on defenseless America when the incensed Italians returned in high dudgeon to Rome.

Everything had gone as Jimmy Christopher had planned—until suddenly a shot rang out almost at his ear, and the head of a German agent was outlined above the ridge of the roof, his body on the other slope. Too late Jimmy realized that the Germans had not left those rooftops entirely unguarded.

The fellow's Luger came up again, aiming carefully. His eyes gleamed triumphantly. Jimmy knew there was no time to flee or even to dodge; he would be shot down, sent somersaulting four stories to the rear courtyard. But at that instant the German's gun swiveled and barked. The bullet hit its mark; smashed home in Bill Hubert's shoulder—Hubert, who had caught the steel ladder's grappling hooks on the roof ridge and was already scrambling up toward Richter's man!

"No, Bill—you can't make it!" Jimmy shouted frantically and started to crawl along the ledge toward the ladder.

But Hubert paid no heed. A second bullet smashed into him, stopped him momentarily—but he went on again inexorably. Now he was within a few feet of the German. The Luger roared almost in his face—but his arms stretched out and his fingers fastened on the fellow's sleeve. Viciously, the German swung his weapon, using it as a club, pounding savagely at Hubert's unprotected head.

Jimmy now saw the blood stream from Hubert's battered, unprotected head....

Jimmy also saw the blood come from the side of Bill's face—saw the grim set of his jaws, the glare of his eyes. Bill Hubert was like a madman—and looked like a dead man. A man dead on his feet but still clinging to an inflexible purpose!

His arms wrapped around the German, his legs entwining the man's body. For a moment they swayed dizzily there on the ridge—and then they lost their balance! Rolling and pitching, they plunged down the steep roof, bounced off its edge—and catapulted into the street below! Wild terror keened in a piercing shriek from the German's throat... but not a sound came from Bill Hubert's tightly clenched lips as he plummeted to his death!

Jimmy Christopher had been almost within reach of the struggling men just as they lost their balance—had almost grabbed Hubert's coat as they slid down the roof. Shaken and weak with horror, he watched that fatal plunge... then crawled slowly, heavily, back to the ledge and finished his precarious journey. Safe at last in his destination apartment, he quickly donned his new disguise, worked over his face, and then took his place at the window beside the dummy that should have been Bill Hubert.

Down in the street the police had managed to restore order. Bruno Caesar's car was still there, a safe distance from the buildings that line only one side of the Ringstrasse, flanked now by his own bodyguard and a phalanx of German troopers. Franz Schnabel had also arrived. Through the crowd pressed a man Jimmy recognized as Kurt von Richter, behind him two others carrying a body—Bill Hubert's bone-shattered corpse. Straight to Schnabel they took it, and in that moment Operator 5 knew that he had lost. Bill Hubert's glorious sacrifice had been in vain....

Hard-eyed, grim-jawed, he watched while Richter exposed Hubert's masquerade, and the evidence was presented to Bruno Caesar. Heart-sick, he listened as the public address system blared forth the discovery and then resounded with the voices of Franz Schnabel and Bruno Caesar as they clasped hands and cemented their pact.

Operator 5 had failed—and the fate of America was sealed!

CHAPTER 9
CONQUERED CHATTELS

IT WAS nightfall three days after the signing of the Italo-German alliance when a road-dusty traveler cycled up to an inn on the main street of the little Alpine village of Mallerkirchen. Wearily, he glanced about him and eyed the two young countrymen sitting at a side table as he strode up to the desk. He signed the register, *August Schrender* after he had scrutinized it carefully through his silver-rimmed spectacles. August Schrender, a chemist from Hamburg out on a bicycling vacation, was what he told the landlord.

When his host had shown him upstairs to his room, Operator 5 tiptoed to the door and waited until the old man's footsteps had again clumped down the flight. Then he stepped noiselessly into the hallway and listened at the head of the stairs. All seemed normal in the public rooms below. There was no whispering—no suspicious hush. Apparently, he had not been trailed this far, and the landlord had not had his suspicions aroused.

For three days Jimmy Christopher had been hounded from place to place by Richter's agents. Twice he had managed to elude them only by a wide swing to the north. But always he had headed back into the Tyrol—back toward the lofty mountain retreat where Franz Schnabel often went for rest and for his most important private conferences.

Much had happened during those three days. With clockwork precision the plans for the conquest of America had gotten underway almost the moment the concord between Germany and Italy was signed. The very next day the Italian navy had started convoying transports loaded with Roman legions across the Atlantic—and the invasion Operator 5 had tried so desperately to prevent had definitely begun.

With his plans crumbling dismally around his ears, Jimmy had grasped at the only straws that remained. Proof of Franz Schnabel's perfidious intentions—that was the one slim hope of halting those legions before helpless America was once more laid waste and enslaved. And the most likely place such proof might be secured was from the arrogant *Reichsfuehrer*—from Franz Schnabel himself!

To attempt to reach Schnabel in Berlin would be worse than futile; it would be useless suicide. But when he was in his closely guarded Alpine retreat there would be at least a chance of finding a means of access to him.

Jimmy Christopher did not delude himself about the slimness of that chance or about the risk he was running. All he asked was an opportunity to stake his life on a desperate gamble—and, if it failed, a chance to follow Hubert, Ellis, Insley, Baxter and all that gallant company who had gone uncomplainingly down the death trail Howard Thorne had blazed.

And now Jimmy was there, in the Mallerkirchen inn—with Franz Schnabel less than a mile away, in the modernized castle that looked down on the picturesque village below....

Wearily, Jimmy washed his hands and face and brushed the dust from his clothing. But, as he worked, his vigilant ears were strained to catch the slightest suspicious sound. Suddenly he stopped, tiptoed closer to the door and put his ear against the panel. Up from the downstairs rooms came new sounds—a girl's half-strangled scream, and then loud, raucous laughter, thick-tongued German taunts.

"Nein—nein!" the girl pleaded fearfully. "You mustn't do that to me! Oh, please—"

The frightened words died on her lips, were smothered by a gasp of pain, and then by coarse, brutal laughter. Now Jimmy could make out the sounds of a struggle. He could hear the girl trying to run out of the room and, apparently being cornered, loose her outraged protests as the man overpowered and mauled her.

Bucolic German love-making, he shrugged—yet there was a note of horror, of utter wretchedness, in her voice that stabbed at him. That and something more.... Somehow, her accent didn't ring true—didn't have the guttural thickness of native Germans....

CURIOUSLY, HE eyed the horseplay as he went downstairs and took a seat at a side table, to order a *seidel* of beer. While the anxious-faced girl waited on him, they let her alone. But as soon as she was finished one of the young huskies grabbed her and pulled her toward him. Twisting her arm up behind her back cruelly, he forced her head down until it was at the level of his partner's face. Then he compelled her to remain there while the fellow slobbered kisses over her, a hell of shame and despair flaring in her agonized eyes.

"So you don't want to kiss me, eh?" The amorous swain drew back angrily. "You're too good for kisses, eh? Well, it's time you were taught something. *Herr* Schroeder has been too easy with you. I'll soon teach you how to kiss!"

Yanking her away from his companion, he leered significantly in the direction of the stairway and began to drag her toward it.

"*Nein! Nein!*" she panted frantically. "*Herr* Schroeder will be very angry! He will—"

"He will do nothing!" her captor jeered—but at that moment she broke away from him, left part of her dress in his clawing hands as she sprang clear and glanced around the room like a trapped animal.

A moment of indecision—and then straight toward Jimmy Christopher she ran. But the German caught up with her in two strides, swept out his hand and slapped it brutally against the side of her face. Headlong she pitched across the floor, almost at Jimmy's feet, and lay whimpering there as the bully came to grab her.

But that was all Jimmy could stand.

"Let her be!" he commanded gruffly. "The girl is hurt."

For an amazed moment the lumbering countryman stared at him, cheeks flushing and eyes narrowing angrily. His big hands drew back threateningly—but before he could make a hostile move Jimmy was out of the chair and his fist lashed upward in a perfectly coördinated knockout uppercut. That blow lifted the bully off his feet, slammed him back against the wall, breathless and glassy-eyed, just as his partner came charging in like a rushing bull—only to be grasped by the wrist and pin-wheeled through the air. Right over Jimmy Christopher's head he traveled—to land in a heap on top of his blinking, groaning mate.

BRUNO CAESAR

KURT RICHTER

FRANZ SCHNABEL

DR. OLIVER

By now *Herr* Schroeder had appeared on the scene and quickly grasped the situation. Gruffly, he ordered the girl out of the room and then scolded the two countrymen, who now sulked on their stools and eyed Jimmy covertly—as if they could not quite understand what had happened.

That seemed to be all of it. A short while later they left, and half an hour after that Jimmy went up to his room. For a long while sleep would not come to him. The inn noises quieted, the lights went out, and everyone seemed to be asleep. Everyone but he—and someone who was suddenly tapping on his door!

Instantly, Jimmy was out of bed, his automatic ready in his hand. Cautiously, he opened the door—and was amazed to see the frightened face of the inn slavey peering in at him.

"Please, may I come in?" she whispered—in English! And then, when he had drawn her inside and closed the door after her, "You *are* an American, aren't you? I knew you must be the way you fought for me. Nobody else would do that for—"

"Who are you?" Jimmy demanded, still suspicious that this might be more of Richter's trickery.

"Martha Dayton—I used to live in Marietta, Ohio," she told him quickly. "My family was wiped out in the invasion, and I was captured by *Herr* Schroeder's son. He brought me back here when Emperor Rudolph was killed. It has been terrible—working like a slave, and taking all their filthy abuse. I can't stand any more of it!"

Sobs shook her overworked young body. Jimmy Christopher patted her shoulder comfortingly, while his heart went out to her—one of the many thousands of American prisoners who had been dragged off to Europe to become slaves, mere chattels of their owners, by the retreating troops of the Purple Empire. She had been abused and beaten, made to work like an animal—and yet they had not been able to break her spirit.

Perhaps she was that one slim chance in a thousand....

"Yes, I am an American," Jimmy told her quietly. "Men call me Operator 5—"

"Operator 5!" The girl's hand flew to her lips to smother the startled exclamation that almost burst from them. "I know about you! My brother saw you once—before we lost track of him. There must be some reason for you being here," she divined quickly. "Something to do with this new war they are starting?"

Jimmy Christopher studied her searchingly. In her pale, tragic-eyed face he read no guile, nothing but pathetic delight at having met a fellow-American—and a fervent desire to be of help. Quickly, he told her what had happened, outlined his mission, the forlorn hope that had brought him to Mallerkirchen. Then he waited. For a moment she was silent, while her dark eyes glowed and sparkled with excitement. Then her hand was on his arm, her fingers gripping him tensely.

"I know someone who may be able to help!" she whispered. "Someone who goes up there to the castle. Harvey Sawyer—he's one of us—a prisoner from America. He belongs to Ludwig Taube, the grocer, and he takes a load of supplies up to the castle twice a week. Tomorrow is his day!"

"Tomorrow?" Jimmy glanced at his watch. "But it is nearly eleven o'clock. Tonight it is too late—"

"No," Martha Dayton interrupted eagerly. "It isn't too late.

109

Now is a good time, when they have all gone to sleep. Harvey sleeps in a little room over the store. I can wake him by throwing pebbles against his window—that's a way we have. I can take you there now."

Noiselessly, Jimmy followed her down the stairs and out through the rear of the inn. By back alleys she led the way to Taube's grocery, tossed up half a dozen pebbles at the window above it—and soon Harvey Sawyer came poking his head warily out of the back door.*

Like Martha Dayton, he was gaunt and undernourished, but a man of about Jimmy's size and build. Wide-eyed, he listened while Operator 5 outlined the plan that had been quickly taking form in his mind. Wide-eyed and trembling—but his jaws clenched grimly and his hands balled into tight fists.

"I'm a coward, Operator 5," he whispered the abject admission. "I was a pacifist—because I was afraid to fight. When the Purple armies swept through *my* home town—little Bellows Falls, Vermont—I was captured because I had stayed home with the old men who couldn't fight. But I am all over that now. All that I ask is a chance to do my part—just a chance to make up to America for my slacking. You can count on me to do anything you say!"

---

* Author's Note: It may seem strange that American slaves in Europe were not more closely guarded and confined, but the reader must take into consideration their utter helplessness. They had no means of flight, or even of existence, should they attempt to run away. Moreover, in Germany such attempts were punishable by death.

THE NEXT morning the heavily loaded, oxen-drawn truck pulled away from the store of *Herr* Taube as usual and plodded slowly up the steep hill to the castle where Europe's most ambitious dictator sat dreaming of world conquest. At the gate the sentries nodded in response to his mumbled, *"Gut Morgen,"* and the bobbing of his feathered-capped head, then swung back the barrier and allowed him to pass on to the kitchens at the rear of the miniature fortress. There he climbed down and hitched the team, starting to unload and carry the heavy boxes and bags into the storeroom. But as he worked he was aware of the suspicious scrutiny of an old, bearded peasant who was sweeping up the yard.

Half a dozen times he caught the oldster peering at him suspiciously, and then the fellow shuffled closer and eyed him deliberately, shook his head satisfiedly. There was something very familiar about that dirty, heavily whiskered face—but before Operator 5 had time to place it, the old man was speaking to him in a dull, vacuous voice.

"You're not Taube's man." He shook his grizzled head wisely. "I can tell. You can't fool me. The way you tie the oxen—he never does it that way. And the way you carry those heavy boxes— sometimes I have—have to help him get them off the truck. No, you're not Taube's man. I'm going to tell the *Herr* Hauptmann—"

He started toward the quarters of the guard, but Jimmy Christopher sprang after him, grabbed him by the sleeve—only to find that the fellow had surprising strength. Tearing loose, he backed away and opened his mouth to yell for help—but then Jimmy was on him in earnest. Catching the old fellow in a headlock, he dropped him to the ground with stunning force and leaped astride him, fingers tight in his throat choking back the strangled outcry before it could reach his lips.

Helpless, the clean-up man lay there without attempting to struggle. That fall seemed to have taken all the fight out of him; seemed almost to have paralyzed him. Jimmy saw his eyes bulging from his head, saw his lips moving soundlessly—and then suddenly he wrenched clear long enough to find his voice.

"Jimmy!" gasped from him before his throat was again imprisoned.

Jimmy.... Operator 5 relinquished the pressure of his fingers the slightest degree and stared down into the old man's face. Now the dull, half-witted look had gone out of the blue-gray eyes. Intelligence had flashed back into them—intelligence and recognition.

Impossible that this man could be—

Incredulously, Jimmy Christopher stared into those now familiar eyes, saw beneath the dirt and grime, beneath the rank growth of whiskers—*and recognized his own father!* John Christopher, whom he had given up for dead since an early wave of the Purple Invasion had overwhelmed him and supposedly wiped him out!

"It's true, Jimmy," John Christopher's bearded lips murmured as the pressure on his throat relaxed. "It's a long story—seems ages and ages since I was shot down and captured by Rudolph's men. They kept me as a slave behind the lines and finally brought me to Europe. Most of the time I have been helpless—a stupefying coma seemed to come over me, and I was like an automaton. There have been three years of that—three years of darkness, with only occasional flashes of horrible understanding. But now you have come for me—that's why you are here, Jimmy?"

Operator 5 had lifted him to his feet and drawn him to the side of the truck, where he pretended to be working over the harness of the oxen. Swiftly, he outlined the story of the past three years and told his father why he was there—and, as he listened, the man who had once been Operator Q-6 of American Intelligence nodded his head in quick understanding.

"The problem is to overpower Schnabel," he pondered. "But he is guarded so carefully—"

"Not necessarily to overpower him—just to overhear him; to catch him making admissions that will confirm what I believe," said Jimmy. "If I could get into his rooms, I have a dictograph all ready to be installed."

Now John Christopher's eyes were flashing excitedly. For years before the Purple Invasion he had had to lead a quiet life, careful that he did not over-exert himself for fear of the bullet that was lodged close to his heart and might mean his death at any time—but now he was back in harness, back in the perilous game that had been his life-work.

"I can locate that for you," he planned swiftly. "It is part of my work to empty the spittoons and sweep his rooms. I should be at it now. I know a place where I can hide the instrument in his study—the room he uses as an office. Of course, I won't be able to conceal the wire very well—it will have to hang out the window. That will be dangerous—"

"Where can you hide me?" Jimmy snapped eagerly.

"In my room, down there beside the kitchens," his father supplied promptly. "It will be easy to lead the wire there—but the question is: how can we get you back through the gate after you drive out?"

"I'm not driving out," Operator 5 grinned. "My double is doing that—" and he lifted a corner of the truck's tarpaulin to reveal Harvey Sawyer crouching there, ready to step out and take his place on the driver's seat!

CHAPTER 10
AMERICA IS DOOMED!

HAD ANYONE watched Ludwig Taube's truck he might have noticed that the driver carried a sack of coffee into the castle storeroom and did not come out—until he appeared to be suddenly miraculously back on the seat, stepping down to untie the oxen. But nobody was watching that closely—nobody gave the truck a second glance as it lumbered through the gateway and started down the hill....

Nobody but the two Americans who waited tensely in the barely furnished cubby-hole that was the menial "Johann's" bedroom.

"So far so good," John Christopher murmured as he heard the gate clang shut. "Now, if I can have a few moments alone in Schnabel's study...."

When he shuffled into the *Reichsfuehrer's* rooms the dictograph was tucked under his soiled blouse—and five minutes later its wire was trailing down the side of the building, to be caught and drawn tight through a window of his bedroom. There Jimmy took up his tense vigil, the earphones clasped to his head and the recorder ready to be set in operation the moment Schnabel's voice came over the wire.

Long, seemingly endless hours he sat there, fearful at every moment that some alert eye would discover the telltale wire and bring Richter's men swarming down upon him. Long, tedious hours, while the slim hope for American freedom hung precariously in the balance—but at last there was the sound of footsteps in Schnabel's study, and then the rumble of his voice!

"Good—good!" he was chuckling as he plumped his heavy bulk into his desk chair. "All is good—everything goes as we planned!"

"Everything, *Excellenz,*" another voice agreed unctuously— the unmistakable voice of Kurt von Richter! "The latest reports from America are extremely satisfactory. Our agents have been very successful in recruiting the men of the Purple armies who still hold Canada—and there will be an army of nearly fifty thousand trained warriors waiting for Marshal Rinaldi even before his own legions arrive. Our forces, as you know, are converging at a point above North Dakota—where our 'allies' behind the American defense line have everything in readiness."

"Good—very good!" Schnabel chuckled again. "Rinaldi should be there in four or five more days—and then we will be ready!"

"The mobilization—it is completed?" Richter asked diffidently.

"Perfectly," the Reichsfuehrer enthused. "And Bruno Caesar knows—that is the finest part of it. He thinks our armies are ready to sweep across Belgium and Holland and throw a scare into England. But the moment I give the word they will storm through the Brenner Pass, while our bombers fly thousands of machine-gun units into the very heart of the country. In less than a week, Italy will be ours from one end to the other—and then all Europe will be at our feet!" His breathing was jerky.

"They begrudged us the colonies that were rightfully ours," he flared, "and now we will take a colony that is worthwhile—a colony where we can build a new *Reich!* All of America will be ours, from the Atlantic to the Pacific, from the Arctic to Panamá—but we shall not be so foolish as Emperor Rudolph and his stupid advisers. They lost everything, even their lives, because they tried to force the stiff-necked Americans to do their will."

He went on. "No, I shall not make that mistake. Instead of trying to conquer them I will annihilate them! I want the American continent—not the American people, because they will never make good subjects. We will wage against them the same sort of extermination campaign they used so effectively on their own Indians. Wipe them out—that is the plan. Exterminate all but those we want to keep as slaves—and these will be herded onto closely guarded reservations in the wastes of Canada."

Bitterly, Jimmy Christopher cursed the deluded Dr. Oliver as he listened to that program of cold-blooded mass slaughter. The poor, blind fool, dazzled by the tinsel glamor of Fascism, was dooming his country and his own companions to destruction!

Instead of the overlordship of America which they expected would be theirs, death was the reward Franz Schnabel would hand out to those traitorous renegades!

"And you, my dear von Richter," the satisfied voice of the dictator rang in Operator 5's ears, "for your excellent services in America, you will be appointed governor-general of the conquered territory. You will have the task of rebuilding it properly, so that it will become a source of wealth and power to the Fatherland."

His voice rose. "Germany the undisputed master of Europe, from the Arctic to the Mediterranean, and with all the resources of the American continent at our command—that will be world dominion, my dear van Richter!" he cried. "A dream I have long cherished, and now it is about to be realized. Now there remains only—?"

Suddenly, Jimmy tensed, and the words coming over the wire were drowned by a commotion just outside the window. A loud, angry voice shouting abuse—and then the resounding crack of a brutal, flogging blow that was echoed by a low groan of pain.

"Lazy *Lümmel!*" the guttural voice. "I have watched you wasting time when there is work to be done. Loafing around here in the courtyard—waiting for a chance to sneak off into your room and go to sleep! I will teach you—"

The angry shouting stopped abruptly, as if the speaker was too amazed to continue. A moment of stunned silence—and then....

"What is this? A wire! A *wire* that goes into your room—and runs upstairs to the quarters of the *Fuehrer!*"

THE EARPHONES were snapped from Jimmy's head

117

as the dictograph wire was seized from outside and yanked savagely. Just in time, he grabbed the recorder and snatched the precious record that might mean life or death for millions of people thousands of miles away. Tucking it securely under his blouse, he bent close to the curtained window—and saw John Christopher lying on the ground as the uniformed palace majordomo stood over him and lashed at him furiously with a leather whip.

"So you are trying to spy!" the outraged official roared. "Spying on the *Fuehrer!*"

Helplessly, the old man cowered on the pavement and tried to protect his face from the whistling lash. But at the word "spy," men seemed to come running from every direction. Uniformed hussars from the gate, servants from inside the building—and two grim-faced civilians whom Jimmy recognized as members of Richter's secret police.

In another minute, they would be outside the room, would have him trapped, cut off—would find that priceless record and confiscate it or smash it to bits. But Operator 5 did not wait for that. Stepping quietly into the short, semi-dark corridor, he catfooted to the door and suddenly flung it open. In a bound he was alongside the majordomo, his automatic arcing down on the fellow's skull just as that flailing whip wrung another groan from its cringing victim.

John Christopher had suffered cruelly, but he was watching alertly—was on his feet in an instant, racing behind Jimmy as his son led the way across the courtyard. Twice Jimmy's Luger roared—and Kurt von Richter's agents pitched to the ground before they could fire a shot.

But already others were taking their places, and Jimmy knew that it was hopeless to try to make a stand. There was only one possibility of escape—one slim chance.

Racing across the courtyard and to one side of the main building, he spied a two-story structure that looked like a garage. A garage that should have cars in it. If he was wrong they would be hopelessly trapped once they reached that building—but there was no choice. Bullets whistled around them as they ran, thudded into the wide doors as they flung them open—and Jimmy almost whooped with relief. There were two big cars in the garage—and the keys had been left in one of them!

"Hold them off, Dad!" he snapped as he thrust the Luger into John Christopher's hand and leaped behind the wheel. Desperately, he toed the starter and threw the powerful Daimler into gear. Beside him the Luger roared, and he caught a glimpse of a man toppling off the running-board—of another sprawling on his face in the doorway. And then the car was gathering speed as it rolled across the courtyard toward the gateway.

The sentries at the entrance saw them too late to close the open gates. They made a desperate try; but John Christopher shot one of them down, and the other dived out of the way as the car hurtled straight at him—only to swing sharply to one side when a crash seemed inevitable and dart through the gate. BRAKES MEANT nothing to Operator 5 right now. Wildly, he tore down the hill at a pace none of Franz Schnabel's drivers would dare attempt. He had a start—a few precious seconds—but there were other cars up there at the castle that would soon be following him, and his task was not finished. There was still a promise to be kept.

On two wheels the heavy machine swung around to the side of Ludwig Taube's market, brakes screaming a shrill protest as it drew up at the rear—and *Herr* Taube gasped in amazement as his clerk leaped from behind the counter and dashed out to one of *Reichsfuehrer* Schnabel's own cars!

That car stopped once more, in front of the Mallerkirchen inn, and Martha Dayton came running toward it eagerly—was grasped and pulled inside before the Daimler had lost momentum. Like a relieved racer, the machine picked up speed and headed toward the west—the first lap in the long, hazardous journey back to America!

The pursuit was hot on their heels even before they were out of the village, but the fleet Daimler had little difficulty maintaining its lead, then widening it until the trailing cars were completely outdistanced. Outdistanced, but not shaken off—Jimmy knew that they would come on doggedly. Richter would be flashing the news ahead, pitting the way with traps and ambuscades.

At Hof Gastein there was a barrier piled across the road, but Jimmy stepped on the gas and the Daimler went through it like a battering-ram. At Krimml a police car darted out and sped along beside them the moment they appeared. Shots blasted from it and bullets poured into the Daimler, but John Christopher returned that fire coolly and with deadly effectiveness. In less than half a mile the police car swerved, cut crazily across the road and piled up in a ditch.

Operator 5's eyes had been glued to the road, but from their corners he had been watching Harvey Sawyer, on the seat beside him. Sawyer, too, clutched an automatic that Jimmy had given him, but he held it as if it were a lighted bomb. When he fired, it was with his eyes nearly closed and with fingers that trembled like those of an ague-sufferer. The man's face was almost green with fear.

"Watch him, Jimmy," John Christopher warned at the first opportunity. "He's a weakling. He can't help it—he's just built that way."

Outside Innsbruck they deserted the Daimler and hid by the side of the road, while Jimmy went into town and bought changes of clothing. That ruse kept them safe for the night, but in the morning Richter's agents were combing the town and arresting everyone who was not a native of the place.

BARELY, IN time, Jimmy got his party out of town in a farmer's milk truck. After that their slow progress across Germany was a desperate game of hide and seek, with Death the grim searcher. That trip took them more than a week instead of the twenty-four hours it should have consumed—but at last they were across the border and had reached Paris. There they hid away in rooms in a little *pension* on the Rue Jacob—top-floor rooms, so that they could take to the roofs if the police or Richter's agents blocked escape by the hall.

At last the final details were arranged. Jimmy had booked steerage passage for four French emigrants bound for America, and the next morning they would board the boat-train for Cherbourg. Then, only the width of the Atlantic—and that incriminating dictograph record would be on American soil, speeding to Marshal Rinaldi's headquarters....

Aglow with his good news, Jimmy Christopher climbed to the top floor of the *pension,* started down the gloomy hallway—and almost fell over a figure huddled on the floor. It was the body of a man! One of Richter's agents, Jimmy quickly identified him—and marveled to see that, although the fellow still clutched a Luger, he had been choked to death, his throat torn and bloodied where savage fingers had ripped deep into it!

Not a sound came from the rooms where John Christopher and the others should be waiting. Tingling with apprehension, Jimmy dashed to the door and threw it open—to stare in amazement at the scene which confronted him in the disordered room!

John Christopher and Martha Dayton sat, bound and gagged, on a couch—and on the floor in front of them lay the bodies of two men locked in a death-grapple. They were the bodies of another of Kurt Richter's agents—and Harvey Sawyer!

Two bullets, fired close against Sawyer's body, had blasted the life out of him—but not before his tearing fingers had choked the German agent to death. Jimmy bent over the tangled bodies and could hardly pry those constricted fingers from their clutching hold. Pityingly he looked into Sawyer's still face—and saw that it was alight with exultation.

"Two of those fellows jumped Martha and me," old John Christopher explained as soon as his mouth was freed of the gag. "They came in through the window of the next room. Then they tied us up and sat down to wait for you and Sawyer to get back. One of them went outside, when he heard Harvey coming—and you saw what happened to him!"

"And then Harvey came in here," the girl marveled softly. "He could have escaped; he could have gone off and left us, but he heard this fellow call out to his partner. He came in to save us—" There were tears in her eyes, but they were shining with a new pride—and as Jimmy looked down on that exultant face he mutely apologized to Harvey Sawyer for the disparaging thoughts he had entertained. Sawyer had been no fighter; he had not even the instinct to grab the automatic from the hand of the man he had downed in the hallway—but he had walked in there barehanded to what he must have known would be his death.

Harvey Sawyer had been what men call a coward—but as Jimmy tenderly lifted his corpse to the settee the dead lips seemed to whisper that, no matter how overwhelming the odds, America never could be conquered while she had "cowards" such as this!

CHAPTER 11
THE MARK OF JUDAS

SEVEN WEEKS had brought new furrows to the brow of Triumvir Warren, had turned his iron-gray hair a shade whiter—as well they might. Those weeks had been ones of ceaseless worry and alarm in Washington, of feverish hoping and endless waiting.

At first Operator 5 had managed to send guarded messages

from abroad, but then the reports had ceased and he and his courageous band were blanketed with silence so complete that it seemed the tomb must have closed upon them. At home the situation was equally bad. Dozens of American Intelligence men had gone into North Dakota—and none of them had returned. They had been swallowed up by that great wasteland that was claiming trainload after trainload of supplies—that had ambushed and wiped out a column of troops sent to locate and bring in the thieves.

Somewhere in that almost impenetrable desolation Dr. Oliver was sitting like a poisonous spider in the center of his web, waiting for the moment when he and his renegade outfit would be ready to strike. Triumvir Warren knew that, but there seemed to be nothing he could do about it. Like Damocles sitting beneath the sword, he knew that the storm would break at any hour, any minute—if it had not broken already....

Beside his desk sat a bright-eyed, yellow-haired young woman whose attractive features strikingly resembled those of the one who had sat in that chair seven weeks before. Nan Christopher was Operator 5's twin sister—his "other self," as he sometimes called her. Now her rich red lips were tight-pressed, her blue eyes worried.

"It is nearly two months since Di and Tim Donovan disappeared up there," she gave voice to the very thought that was at that moment in Warren's mind. "General Ferrara thinks they are dead—but I don't believe that. Somehow, I *feel* that they are alive. I can't stand this waiting any longer, Mr. Triumvir. I am going up there to find them." Her lips were set.

"Jimmy would do that, if he were here," she said softly, "and one thing he taught me is to carry on when he is away. Even after he may be—gone. He would not sit around here and wonder what is happening out there in the Dakotas—and I won't either."

Andrew Warren made an attempt to dissuade her, but his protests were half-hearted, so desperately was he in need of news. Willingly would he have gone himself, if that were possible. But his was the task of sitting and waiting—of nerve-wracking fretting and dreading what each hour might bring forth....

Nan Christopher stopped at the airline office and made a reservation for the one o'clock plane for Chicago, but her trip seemed to be ill-fated from the start. Half a dozen little things went wrong and delayed her so long that, when her taxi rushed up to the airport, she was just in time to see the plane taking off.

Disconsolately, she stood biting her lip and watching the ship fade into the blue of the sky—but before it was out of sight she tensed and stared open-mouthed. Something was wrong up there. Smoke was trailing from the tail... then suddenly the whole plane blew apart, like a skyrocket ball exploding as it reached the apex of its flight!

"Gawd, lady—your luck's sure with you today!" the taxi-man marveled, as he gaped at the catastrophe. "A couple minutes sooner and you'd have been on that plane!"

Luck was all that had saved her, Nan admitted—saved her from something that she was not at all sure was an accident. The way that ship had completely disintegrated suggested an infernal machine—a deadly destroyer that was set in operation by the plane's own motor....

"You gonna stay here and wait for another plane—after *that?*" The chauffeur was incredulous. "Me—I'm cured o' them things for life!"

But Nan did wait for the next plane. She had the airport manager point it out to her and kept her eyes on it all afternoon. When it finally took to the air she knew that nobody had had an opportunity to tamper with it. Without a sign of trouble it rose from the field and gained altitude, then straightened out on its westward course... and she began to think that perhaps her suspicions were merely imaginary.

By the time she reached Chicago and alighted she had almost become lulled—when suddenly a plane rushed out of the night and nearly decapitated her before she was off the field! Only by throwing herself flat on the ground did she manage to save herself. Then she caught the barely audible popping of a muffled automatic as the turf kicked up around her and spattered sand squarely in her face! Now there was no longer any doubt. Dr. Oliver's agents knew her identity and her mission, and did not intend to let her accomplish it. After that, her vigilance was untiring, her eyes darting glances everywhere about her, ears strained for the slightest warning sound.

IT WAS that vigilance that saved her life the next morning as she drove up to one of the division headquarters of the Ferrara Line. Dismissing her driver, she started to walk toward the squat headquarters building, interestedly observing the beehive activity all around her, when she heard her name being called discreetly. Surprised, she hesitated.

"Miss Christopher!" it came again—and then she located the man who was hailing her.

It was an overall-clad worker in the railroad yard adjoining the headquarters building. He was standing behind a freight car, careful that no other workers could see him.

"Just a moment, before you go inside," he called softly. And then, "It's about Tim and Miss Elliot," as she still hesitated.

Tim and Diane! Quickly, Nan started toward him—started to pick her way across the maze of tracks toward the spur behind which he was standing. The fellow seemed to be afraid of being seen talking to her, but he knew something about Tim and Diane—perhaps where they were being held captive, or where—

That was the moment her alert ears snatched her from the open jaws of death! A sound, barely noticeable, off there to her right—a low rumble that seemed to be bearing down upon her. And then the track she was crossing *vibrated* as she touched it. Just in time, her quick mind correlated those two—and she leaped clear, to fall flat on the cinder-strewn ground beside the track as a big freight car rolled past her. Apparently escaped from a string at the other end of the slightly inclined spur, the car had gathered momentum as it bore down upon her, a silent juggernaut that would have pinned her beneath its grinding wheels—

Fifty feet past her that car was rent asunder by a terrific explosion that tore the entire forward end of it into kindling!

Stunned, Nan lay where she had fallen and stared at that dust-shrouded wreckage—realizing the utter fiendishness of the trap she had so narrowly escaped! Knocked down and pinned even momentarily beneath the wheels of that car, she would have been directly under that deadly blast!

A feeling of weakness surged over her at the thought—and then men were running toward her from all directions. Workers and soldiers gathered around her and were lifting her to her feet when an officer pushed his way through them.

"Dan—Dan Porter!" Nan gasped as she recognized him. "I heard there was a Colonel Porter in charge here—but I didn't realize it was you, Dan."

"You're not hurt, Nan?" Porter's eyes were frightened and he was all concern until he saw that she was unharmed. Then the fear in his dark pupils subsided, was hidden by a veil of cynicism. "No, I don't suppose you ever expected that I could rise to the exalted rank of colonel," he muttered as he led the way to his headquarters.

"I didn't mean it that way, Dan," Nan Christopher protested. "I only meant that it hadn't occurred to me that you and this Colonel Porter were the same."

That sounded clumsy and inadequate, and for a moment she felt embarrassed. It wasn't fair of Porter, she rebelled; he was deliberately being churlish and disagreeable. But he had always been that way—always touchy and ready to take offense at the drop of a hat.

For a short time, a year before, Daniel Porter had been one of Nan's most attentive admirers. She had liked him genuinely— but she had loved Captain Aloysius MacTavish, a gallant Canadian who had joined forces with Operator 5 and then gone to his death surrounded by a horde of savage Mongols. After her engagement to MacTavish, Dan Porter had disappeared, cutting himself off from her entirely.

"I heard about MacTavish, of course," he said without looking at her. "I'm sorry. He was a good man—and one who got the breaks—until that happened. This life of ours is a mighty queer thing," he switched to cynical observation. "Some men get everything they want almost without lifting a finger for it—love, honor, recognition, promotion, anything a man values. And then there are some of us who work our heads off—and the world just passes us by."

He went on bitterly. "I am one of that sort, Nan. You didn't expect to find me here—a colonel. And yet I fought all through the Purple War. More than once, I saved whole regiments, divisions, from annihilation. Yet men who served under me have risen to be generals—have the very fortifications on which the whole nation depends named after them!"

Daniel Porter was a bitter man—who felt that he had been slighted and that the whole world was against him. Nan Christopher studied his handsome, petulant face and read the discontent that harried him. She set out to overcome that, to win back his good nature—and before the end of the morning his cynicism had vanished, lost in a new concern for her.

"I don't like the idea of you going on along the Line alone," he protested uneasily when they came to the end of his division. "If, as you suspect, there are men here who know what became of Diane Elliot and Tim Donovan, you will be running into danger every foot of the way." He shook his head, frowning.

"Danger here in the Line—with soldiers all around me?" Nan

glanced toward the sentinels on guard at the mouth of every bay in the trenches, the lookouts watching from every eminence. "This should be safe enough for anybody."

"But how about coming back?" Porter worried.

"There probably will be a car coming this way," she shrugged.

But he did not dismiss it that lightly. "It's a dangerous wilderness behind this line, and the roads are impossible," he grumbled. "It would be lots more sensible if you didn't try to go any farther. If you stayed at my headquarters—"

But Nan laughed off his protests and went on her way.

ALL THAT day she worked farther westward, her eyes as alert as her ears as she interviewed officers and men. There was nothing very definite in the information she gleaned, but here and there she did pick up leads. Rumors about strange happenings in the railroad yard where she had almost been killed; hints of suspicious characters who were seen in that sector of the line; veiled insinuations about officers who were too busy being sorry for themselves.

Nothing definite—and yet those straws in the wind all seemed to blow in the direction of Colonel Daniel Porter....

That night Nan spent at a division headquarters near the Montana state line, but early the next morning she was on her way back to Dan Porter's sector. There had been no automobile going in her direction, but one of the officers had offered her the use of his saddle horse, a lively animal that was eager to stretch its legs.

At first Nan was exhilarated by the brisk pace, but as she rode along her thoughts were busy with the disturbing suspicions that had been plaguing her all night—and the going seemed to become slower and slower. Something was wrong up there in Dan Porter's sector; she had sensed it the moment she met him, and now the conviction was almost a certainty.

Something was radically wrong—and that something was coming to a head in the very near future. Undoubtedly, that was why Dr. Oliver's agents had been so anxious to keep her away, so desperate in their attempts to kill her. She had blundered in at an inopportune moment.

Anxiously, she urged the fleet animal on as the long hours past, as the morning yielded to noon. Twelve o'clock—and Nan felt hunger overtake her as she pictured the men up on the Line sitting down for their noon meal. Fifteen or twenty minutes more and she would be with them.

Then she breasted a slightly wooded rise and pulled her mount up short, to stare wide-eyed at a great cavalcade that was winding through the wide draw below. Trucks, wagons, horsemen—an army of black-uniformed men; and they were pushing on toward the Line!

Dr. Oliver's renegades!

For a moment she sat there like a statue, while her impatient mount pawed the ground. Then the animal nickered—and was answered from close at hand!

Instantly, Nan spurred and crouched low over the horse's neck, to dash from that rise just as two black-shirted riders closed in on it. Two more came on from the distance, cutting her off so that she had to turn back. Dodging their bullets, she left the road and took to the open plain, riding off frantically into the wilderness until she dared to swing back once more toward her destination. That detour had cost her precious time—more than ten minutes, she fretted. By now that somber column must be close to the Ferrara Line!

That thought made her desperate, made her throw caution to the wind as she spurred on frantically. At last the buildings behind the Line came in view. There was the railroad yard, Colonel Porter's headquarters—but the black riders were almost up to it. They would reach it before she could get there!

And then she heard the opening salvos from the north—the thunder of big guns and the shriek of shells. The long-expected attack on the Line had begun, timed to the minute to coincide with this traitorous onslaught from the rear!

Feverishly, she quirted the animal, urged it on to its utmost effort. Now those ebon-uniformed renegades saw her, were closing in to cut her off while their bullets rained all around her. This time she did not swerve. With a frantic prayer that the horse would not be hit, she bent low over its mane and galloped straight ahead—right through the cordon that tried to check her, past the deserted railroad yards and headquarters building, and up to the rear entrance to the great Line itself.

Panting, she flung herself from the saddle just as the advance guard of the raiders closed in on her—and as the heavily barred gateway of the Ferrara Line opened wide!

CHAPTER 12
THE DELUGE

N OT UNTIL the *Orleans* cleared the harbor of Cherbourg and steamed out into the English Channel did Operator 5 breathe easily. From a porthole in the steerage of the big liner, he watched the shore of France fade in the distance, and then turned to where his father sat hunched beside Martha Dayton—old Pierre Tussaud with his son Jules and his daughter Denise, according to their passports.

"Six or seven days more," he murmured in the French patios, "but they seem like six or seven centuries!"

The slowly dragging hours seemed even longer the next day when the ship's radio picked up a broadcast from America.

"Apprehension increases hourly in the United States," the voice of the news commentator announced, "as Italian and German troops pour into Canada. Marshal Vittorio Rinaldi is reported to be in command and to have established his headquarters near the ruins of Winnipeg, Manitoba. Estimates of the size of his forces vary, but the combined Italian, German and Purple armies are conservatively conceded to be nearly a quarter million."

The announcer continued. "Although no declaration of war has been made, invasion and the actual beginning of this undeclared war are expected hourly. General Ferrara, in personal command on the Line which bears his name, is mobilizing every available man and calling upon the country for a supreme effort...."

Jimmy Christopher grimly visualized the frantic, hopeless activity along that widespread Line; could visualize the panic that must be sweeping America from coast to coast. No matter how many men he mustered along the Canadian border, Ferrara must know that he could not hope to hold the Line against the onslaught of a quarter million well armed and completely equipped troops. That attack would mean the beginning of the end.

It *must* be stopped—but the only hope of stopping it lay in the carefully packed dictograph record Jimmy guarded every moment.

If only Triumvir Warren and General Ferrara knew that that record was on the way—if only he could get word to them so that they could contact Marshal Rinaldi and spar for time....

The radio was the answer to that problem—a code message to Washington. But Jimmy did not dare approach the operator openly and try to send such a message. Richter's agents might be on board watching for just such a move, and the operator, himself, might be one of them or be in their pay. The risk was too great—and yet that message must be sent.

That left only one course. Jimmy Christopher would have to send it himself, without anyone knowing.

Patiently, he waited until nearly midnight; until the boat was quiet from stem to stern. Cautiously, he and his father climbed to the promenade and boat decks, and then up to the wireless cabin. Stealthily, they approached the lighted deckhouse and crept up to the door. Carefully, Jimmy opened it—to stare down at the bloody corpse of the operator!

The wireless man's skull had been battered in, and his equipment had been ruined—smashed and hacked beyond repair. Cold-blooded murder…but it had effectively silenced the ship's voice for the rest of the trip.

"That means Richter's men are on board," Jimmy whispered as he softly closed the door and started back to the steerage; "and they know or at least suspect, that we are here, too."

CONSTANT VIGILANCE was the rule after that. Martha Dayton insisted on doing her part with the others—taking her turn keeping awake so that never all three slept at once. Half a dozen times Jimmy Christopher's sharp eyes spotted suspicious-looking individuals—strange stewards who were too inquisitive as they worked; visitors from the tourist class who came down to fraternize with friends in the steerage; sightseers from the first class who were being shown through the boat—and scrutinized everything with more than the casual interest such an inspection warranted.

Operator 5 missed none of them, but they seemed unaware of his identity. At least they made no hostile move against him—until the night he stepped out onto the fore deck for a breath of air. Resting his arms on the trail, his eyes peered out into the darkness—out into the west where an imperiled continent lay trembling in fear; where a brutal war machine was being assembled and primed for the bloody slaughter that would mean the end of the world's greatest experiment in democracy.

Fed up with the chafing restrictions and servile obedience of dictator-ridden Europe, Jimmy Christopher longed to fill his lungs with the clean, free air of America—where men dared to think for themselves and dared to print their thoughts on paper so that others might read. Such a land was anathema to Franz Schnabel and all his kind—a government that must be destroyed lest the germs of freedom it engendered should spread to their own down-trodden populations.

But it would *not* be destroyed! Not after Marshal Rinaldi had heard the hypocritical tongue of Franz Schnabel speak from that treachery-revealing record....

Jimmy filled his lungs with the bracing salt air and turned out of the full blast of the wind—just as a shadowy form leaped out of the darkness and pounced upon him. A heavy hand was clapped over his mouth and a knife blade glinted momentarily before his eyes—and then Jimmy Christopher collapsed.

Like a lifeless corpse he slumped to the deck—only to leap from the boards and butt his skull savagely into the face that loomed over him. A groan of agony—and then another attacker leaped in, only to be met by a smash to the jaw that drove him back against the rail. The third came in more warily, circling for an opening to thrust home his knife.

So there were three of them! Like wolves, too avid even to snarl, they came on in a silent, concerted rush. Straight at that third man Jimmy charged. The knife streaked past his face, sank into the muscles of his shoulder. Then he had the grip he sought—a grip that lifted the fellow from his feet and flung him to the edge of the rail, to teeter there for a precarious moment and then disappear overside!

His terrified scream came back thinly, shredded and blown away by the breeze—and before his companions could recover

"If you leave your engines, everyone on this ship will die!"

from their momentary horror, Jimmy was on top of them, pounding his fists into their faces, beating them back, driving them out toward the forepeak. Now their struggle was not so noiseless. One of them reeled and staggered, lost his footing and went down on the deck with a crash.

"What's going on back there?" came a hail from the forepeak as the lookout whirled and snapped his flashlight back over the deck.

That ended the struggle. Instantly the attackers darted to cover, scurried back like rats into their holes, and Jimmy stepped back into the shadow of a winch until he could make his way to a companionway and then on down to the steerage.

AFTER THAT the Christophers stayed off the decks after dark and were wary-eyed when they ventured forth even in daylight. "That won't be the end of it," Jimmy predicted. "They are too desperately anxious to stop that record from reaching Rinaldi. From now on we will be in ever-increasing danger."

But it seemed that he was wrong as the days passed and the shore of America drew steadily closer. The last day arrived—and then the final night. In the morning the already imposing skyline of rebuilding New York would greet them....

Neither Jimmy nor his father slept a wink that night; the danger was too great. They were pretending to read but seeing not a word that was before their eyes when the dread cry of "Fire!" rang through the ship.

"There it is!" Jimmy gritted, as he led the way to the lifeboat to which they had been assigned.

But a single glance at the boat showed that it was useless. The bottom was full of holes, deliberately ruined. The one next in line was as bad. One after the other—ropes slashed, lowering equipment welded tight so that it would not budge, bottoms drilled through or hacked with axes. Every boat on that liner was out of commission—except one that was no longer hanging from its out-turned davits.

"That's the way they left," Jimmy muttered grimly. "They couldn't get the record so they think they will burn it instead. Their job is finished, and we are left here to roast!"

Flames, he could see, were leaping into the night from half a dozen points—incendiary flames fiendishly started where they would do the most harm. Fore and aft the ship was ablaze, and the conflagration was spreading rapidly despite the frantic efforts of the crew to check it. The vessel was doomed—the taut-faced sailors knew that even as they continued the hopeless battle. Afire and completely cut off from the rest of the world by its disabled wireless....

Grim-eyed, Jimmy strode forward and steeled himself to the heartrending misery and terror that confronted him on every side. Through milling throngs of fear-crazed men and women he fought his way to the bridge, where the officers were close to panic.

"Straight ahead!" Operator 5's authoritative voice put an end to their indecision. "Full speed ahead—that is our only hope!"

"If I can keep the engine-room men at their places." The captain nodded worried agreement. "But they are trying to break out and get up on deck. The engineers can't hold them—"

"I can!" Jimmy interrupted—and then he was racing back to

the steerage, to paw through his baggage until he found what he wanted.

The engine-room was in an uproar when he stepped through the doorway. The terrified men were completely out of hand—yapping like a pack of wild beasts at the feet of the officers who were desperately trying to keep them at bay with revolvers.

One of the assistant engineers had already been dragged down into the frenzied pack, and now the men were charging up the ladder to sweep the others out of their way. But they stopped short when Jimmy pushed across the metal platform and confronted them at the top rung—confronted them with something for which they had far more respect than revolvers. A hand grenade! At his back were John Christopher and Martha Dayton with more!

"Stop where you are!" Jimmy shouted down to them, as he threatened to pull the fatal pin. "If you leave your engines, everyone on this ship will die—doomed to be burned to death or drowned. It's much easier to end it this way—and I'll do it if one of you starts up this ladder. You know what these grenades will do if I pull the pins and toss them down there among you—"

One fear-crazed oiler could stand no more. Shrieking wildly, he started for the ladder, utterly mad with terror. But his companions made a dive for him, pulled him back and pinned him to the floor; and then Jimmy knew that he had won. Obediently, they turned and went back to their engines—and that floating furnace plowed steadily toward the American coast.

The engine-room was hot, roasting. Soon it became stifling; the walls like those of an oven, like a furnace. Jimmy felt his senses slipping, felt himself swooning—but held on doggedly. He held on for more than two hours, while men below him dropped prostrate on the floor. Two hours of a literal hell—but when at last he yielded his post and toppled out into the smoke-blackened companionway the *Orleans* was off the eastern tip of Long Island and rescue boats were swarming around her, taking off the surviving passengers and crew.

That precious record was still intact—and Kurt von Richter's last desperate resort to ruthless outrage had failed!

OPERATOR 5 did not take time to go to Washington. As soon as he reached New York, he got in touch with the capital by long-distance telephone. His name was an open sesame past the secretaries and assistants, who shielded overburdened Triumvir Warren from unnecessary interruption—and in a few minutes Warren was at the other end of the line.

"Thank God, Jimmy!" he breathed fervently. "Thank God, you're alive! I had given up hope—"

Swiftly, Jimmy Christopher outlined what had happened; told him of the dictograph record and its momentous message.

"Thank God!" the Triumvir half-whispered again. "We know definitely now that Marshal Rinaldi has established his head-quarters a few miles north of our North Dakota defenses. Get to him as speedily as you can, Jimmy. At any moment I expect to hear that he has started hostilities—but you may be able to reach him first. You've *got* to reach him first, Jimmy—it's our only hope!

"Diane and Tim?" Warren's answer to Jimmy's eager question came soft and reluctant. "There hasn't been a word from them,

Jimmy—not since you left. Your sister started out yesterday to try to locate them."

Nan, too! Jimmy's jaws clenched, and he winced. Now all three of those who were closest and dearest to him were up there in that turbulent wilderness—right in the path of the savage flood that would sweep over America unless he was able to stem it!

From New York Operator 5 commandeered one of the Army's fastest pursuit planes to fly him west; and as he sped toward the danger point on which the eyes of all America were focused his thoughts turned persistently to Diane and Tim Donovan. In Europe they had seemed so far away from him that he could restrain his worry. But now he was home; and they were not there to greet him. For more than eight weeks they had been out there somewhere in the unreclaimed wilderness—whether alive or dead, only those who must have ambushed or captured them could reveal.

They *couldn't* be dead; he would find them somewhere at the end of this long trail. Resolutely, he assured himself of that again and again. But, try as he would, he could not drive away the chill tentacles of fear that fastened around his heart....

It was dusk when he arrived at General Ferrara's headquarters at the Minnesota-North Dakota junction of the Line. Ferrara had already been apprised of his coming and was waiting impatiently for the latest news from Europe, where the radios had been silenced at Franz Schnabel's command. Gaunt-faced, feverish-eyed, the general listened—and called for an orderly even before Jimmy finished.

"You're a godsend, Operator 5!" he exulted. "My scouts tell me that Rinaldi's forces are drawn up all ready to strike—but this will stop them! We'll send a messenger to him immediately."

Quickly, Jimmy Christopher worded the message, and the courier departed to take it over the Line under a flag of truce.

Impatiently they waited for a reply—but two hours passed, and there was no word; nor had the courier returned.

"The greatest troop concentration seems to be farther down the Line, at a point north of where the town of Sarles used to stand," Ferrara explained. "Suppose we go there now and try to contact Rinaldi again when we arrive."

That strange silence from the marshal puzzled and worried Jimmy. He had been so sure of Rinaldi; so certain that the man would keep his word—and yet there was no response after two more couriers had been dispatched from the sector immediately opposite his headquarters. And again neither of the men returned to the Line. "They must have been imprisoned, that's the only answer." Colonel Porter, who was in command at this point, shook his head. "They were two of my best men, thoroughly reliable—"

In the morning three more couriers went over the top, and each of them was thoroughly impressed with the importance of his mission—but that was the last that was seen of them. The enemy lines swallowed them up, and after that there was silence. Rinaldi said not a word, but his silence was eloquent—he had chosen to ignore his bargain....

Anxiously Operator 5 paced the floor—and then reached a desperate conclusion. He would go over himself; would risk taking the precious record with him, to force Rinaldi to listen to it. Then let the marshal try to ignore its perfidity-revealing message! He was won already!

SWIFTLY HE made his preparations—but before he could climb out of the entrenchments thunderous blasts seemed to hurl him back! All along the Line Rinaldi's field guns went into action, hurling tons of iron and steel against the defenders. The earth quivered and trembled under that terrific barrage, and the air was filled with bursting shells. The attack had begun!

Desperately, the inadequately equipped American troops crouched in their trenches and pillboxes, waiting for the onslaught that would sweep up to them the moment that terrific *strafing* ceased. Tense and grim-faced, they waited for what most of them knew must only be death.

Wave after wave of gray-clad, steel-helmeted fighters would storm in upon them, clearing the way with clouds of gas and sheets of sizzling flame; wave after wave to take the place of every one that fell. A hopeless, suicide task… and yet the Americans stood their ground.

Through the defense Operator 5 strode, redistributing the troops, spreading out the ammunition as equally as possible, heartening the desperate men with words of encouragement and an appearance of confidence. That was Colonel Porter's job, but Porter seemed to have disappeared—busy, no doubt, in his headquarters when he should be up there in the trenches where his men could see him. Already his absence was spreading uneasiness among his subordinates; had the men whispering to one another.…

The man was far from an ideal officer, Jimmy decided, as he set out to look for Porter and bring him up where he belonged. But the colonel was not in his headquarters, was not in any of the bays.

Now the ground-shaking thunder was slackening. The boom of the big guns gave way to the chatter of machine-guns—and Jimmy knew that the invaders were coming over the top—wave after wave of them to overwhelm the shaken, half-stunned defenders. Now was the supreme test....

And at that moment he came upon Colonel Daniel Porter—found him in command of a shifty-eyed squad at the rear of the fortifications. Found them opening wide the heavy gates—to let in a swarm of black-uniformed men. Reinforcements!

There seemed to be a thousand or more of them, all well armed and equipped—but instead of taking their places in the Line, they turned viciously on the defenders. Sweeping up traitorously from the rear, they took the harassed patriots utterly by surprise—traitorously stabbed them in the back while they were grappling with overwhelming odds from the front!

This was the cooperation Dr. Oliver had promised, Operator 5 realized bitterly, as he saw the Line crumble—saw the invaders sweep on victoriously and make a bloody shambles of those desperately defended trenches....

CHAPTER 13
ROMAN HOLIDAY

E VERYTHING SEEMED lost in that black moment, the last slim hope blasted. Nothing was left now but to sell his life as dearly as possible. With cold, bitter fury, Operator 5 fought until his automatics were empty, until a rifle butt crashed against his head and dropped him, half-stunned, to the bottom of a trench. Weakly, he got to his hands and knees, expecting to feel the death-thrust of a bayonet; but his adversary had gone on, was battling farther down the trench.

Dizzily, Jimmy crawled into a covered dugout, lay there recovering his strength. As his head cleared, sanity displaced the berserk fury that had made him momentarily a madman—sanity and grim determination.

All was not yet lost. He was still alive, and so was Marshal Rinaldi—and while they both lived they had an appointment to keep!

Jimmy's clearing eyes glanced around the dugout and discovered the body of a dead soldier lying on the floor. That corpse gave him the germ of an idea. Propping it up on a bench, so that it could be seen from the doorway, he went back to the opening and crouched beside it, empty automatic in hand. Patiently, he waited there, long minutes that seemed hours—and then came the footsteps he had anticipated.

In through the doorway thrust a black-capped head, a gleaming bayonet-tipped rifle. Jimmy groaned softly, and the black-uniformed renegade grunted to a companion, stooped and came through the doorway. But before he could straighten Jimmy's automatic came down crushingly on his skull, the rifle was ripped from his hands—and the gleaming bayonet sank to the hilt in the belly of the fellow who came after him!

Quickly Jimmy Christopher dragged the bodies out of the doorway and stripped the uniform from the fellow with the battered skull. Swiftly he slipped out of his own clothing and donned that outfit of dishonor, picked up the bloody-bayoneted rifle and stepped out into the trench.

That section of the Ferrara Line was now a thing of the past. Those defenders who had not died in the trenches were utterly routed, fleeing in disorder before the gray horde that drove mercilessly after them. The battle front was already miles to the south as the tanks and armored cars of the invaders swept them into the conquered territory.

Somewhere in that territory Marshal Rinaldi and his staff must be directing operations, and that was where Jimmy was headed.

For more than an hour he searched for the new headquarters—an hour during which he had all he could do to steer clear of any of that ebony-garbed renegade crew who might have recognized him as an impostor. And when at last he found it a new impasse confronted him. The headquarters tent was guarded not by the Italian troops he had expected, but by Germans—and by two of Kurt von Richter's agents!

Suspiciously Richter's men grabbed him when he tried to gain admittance, demanded to know what he wanted.

"I have a message for Doctor Oliver," Jimmy gambled—

anything to get into that tent. But the Germans grinned derisively and turned him back in the direction he had come.

"Your Doctor Oliver isn't here," they told him. "Keep looking—you ought to find him back there somewhere," as they waved contemptuously to the rear.

"Then the marshal, if I can't locate Doctor Oliver," Jimmy tried desperately. "Let me talk to Marshal Rinaldi." He raised his voice, hoping that it would reach Rinaldi's ears. "I have a message for him—"

But two bayonets were jabbed into his stomach, pushing him relentlessly back as the stolid-faced soldiers drove him off—with a warning from Richter's men that he would be shot if he tried to return.

Three times that afternoon he tried to reach Rinaldi, as headquarters moved forward. But always the alert Germans were there to block every approach—and now Jimmy knew why there had been no reply to his messages to the marshal. Undoubtedly, Rinaldi had never received them; undoubtedly the couriers had been seized and killed or imprisoned by Richter.

That meant that Vittorio Rinaldi had not gone back on his word—that there still was hope, still a chance if only Jimmy could reach him. He must reach him! But that prospect looked darker and darker as the afternoon and night passed. By then the triumphant invaders had swept across the whole state of North Dakota, and the hard-pressed Americans were trying to rally in South Dakota and Minnesota.

MORNING FOUND the Americans desperately digging new entrenchments and speeding every possible reserve to the new line that must be held unless the whole Mississippi Valley was to be yielded to the gray horde. Feverishly, they worked in the breathing spell that occurred, while the invaders consolidated their positions and stopped to celebrate.

Marshal Rinaldi had established his headquarters in the partially rebuilt city of Fargo, and there the victorious legions gathered for a holiday. A Roman triumph it was to be, Operator 5 learned as he mingled with the celebrating troopers—a triumph that was to be featured by a victory parade with all the trappings of ancient Rome brought up to date....

Jimmy had secured a position of vantage when that triumphal procession began. From a window on the second floor of a building opposite the headquarters hotel, that served as a reviewing stand, he looked down on the hotel porch, where Marshal Rinaldi stood surrounded by his staff. At his side was Kurt von Richter, his waxen-featured face a mask of smiling satisfaction. Just behind him stood Colonel Daniel Porter, decked out in an Italian uniform! Dan Porter—*now one of Rinaldi's aides!*

Dan Porter—a traitor! That was why he had opened the gates to Dr. Oliver's renegades. That was why the invaders had known just where to thrust the spearhead of their attack. And that was the leak in the Ferrara Line that had been draining it of supplies.

Jimmy Christopher gripped the automatic in his holster and longed to send a bullet through that traitor's brain—but at that moment the military band that led the parade had reached the reviewers. After it came the swaggering Germans, the preening Italians resplendent in their polished breastplates and roach-

plumed Roman helmets—rank after rank of them, and between the regiments rumbled the tanks and armored cars.

Like the victor's chariots of old, those grim war machines trailed luckless captives behind them. With wrists chained together, and rope halters around their necks, captured American army officers and women walked through the dust while the soldier-thronged sidewalks jeered at them.

Into the midst of the confusion charged
the reformed ranks of the new America!

Burning with indignation, Jimmy Christopher watched that shameful spectacle—and then his eyes almost popped out of his head! There, behind one of the tanks, their heads held proudly in the air, walked Diane and Nan!

Jimmy stared at their bound hands, their ripped blouses, half torn off—at the ropes around their necks. He remembered the fate Franz Schnabel had decreed for all American prisoners! Extermination—unless they were among the unfortunates who would be chosen for the Canadian slave reservations!

Diane and Nan! But there was nothing he could do; nothing but stand there at the window and watch them led past....

Twenty-four hours of grace that celebration afforded the frantically working American defenders, but Jimmy Christopher knew that their frenzied efforts would be useless. In the morning the big guns began to thunder again, the tanks trundled forward, the armored cars rolled close behind them—and the American line gave way.

The hastily constructed barriers were blown to atoms by that merciless barrage; the trenches crumbled and became untenable as the big tanks rumbled over them, straddled them and poured withering death blasts up and down their length. The ill-equipped and outnumbered American troops fought grimly, clung tenaciously to every defendable position until they were blown out of it. But their defeat was inevitable; human flesh simply could not stand against steel and high-power explosives.

Back, back they went—yard by yard, mile by mile—until the retreat threatened to become a rout. Nothing could save them now.... Nothing except the grim determination and unfailing courage of one black-uniformed figure behind the lines of the invaders. Once more the fate of America rested in the hands of Operator 5....

With an aching heart he had watched the opening of that fearful onslaught and realized what it meant. Fervently, he had prayed for a miracle—even though he knew that not even a dozen miracles could enable General Ferrara and his harried troops to hold that line. And then the die had been cast; the American line had been broken, smashed wide open—and the nation lay prostrate before the invader.

Now there remained only one course—and Operator 5 took it.

Straight to Marshal Rinaldi's headquarters he went—furtively, as long as he was able to avoid attracting attention, and then boldly. The guards stepped up to meet him with ready bayonets, Richter's agents springing up at their sides. For an instant Jimmy fumbled in his breast pocket as if seeking a paper—and then he had thrown himself to one side, had grasped one of those bayoneted rifles and ripped it from the surprised guard's hands... to reverse it and lunge at the fellow's mate.

Steel ground against steel, as the bayonets clashed. For a moment they locked, twisted, and then the German's rifle slipped out of his fingers. With a yell of fear he backed away from the thrust that would skewer him—but Jimmy dropped the weapon and darted past him, through the doorway and into the headquarters tent.

MARSHAL RINALDI was in conference with half a dozen of his staff officers, and at the table with them sat Kurt von Richter. Amazed, they glanced up from the outspread map and stared at this unannounced visitor. Slowly surprised recognition began to dawn in the marshal's face.

But Richter was quicker. Gun in hand, he leaped up from

the table as his men came surging through the doorway with a squad of German guards.

"This man is a spy!" he shouted. "He tried to assassinate Bruno Caesar in Vienna, and now he forces his way in here to try to kill the marshal! He is a spy. He wears the uniform of our allies—that is all the evidence we need. Under the articles of war that means death!"

The guards gripped Jimmy's shoulders, grabbed his arms, started to drag him toward the door.

"Marshal Rinaldi!" he shouted desperately. "I want a few words with the marshal. I have the proof—"

But there was so much noise that he could not be heard—deliberate uproar created by Richter and his men. Now the guards had Jimmy half-way through the doorway—when suddenly he gambled with the chance of a quick bullet. Tearing their grasp, he hurled himself back into the tent, dropped to the floor as Richter fired point-blank at him.

"Marshal Rinaldi!" he shouted again. "Your promise! The word you gave me in Munich! I have the proof you demanded!"

Vittorio Rinaldi's eyes opened wide. For a moment he seemed uncertain, and then his hand darted out and grabbed Richter's Lugar, twisted it up so that the bullet that roared from it tore harmlessly through the top of the tent.

"You have that proof, Operator 5?" he asked skeptically. "Not just hearsay—but proof? Where is it?"

"Here!" Out of the compact knapsack that was strapped tight to Jimmy Christopher's back came the dictograph record, and with it a small, partly collapsible machine for playing it. "Here is a record of Franz Schnabel's own voice! His own words will tell you how he is betraying you at this very moment!"

"Lies!" Richter shouted desperately, as his men surged in. "This is nothing but a trick, Marshal. This man is a murderer—"

"He shall be heard," Rinaldi ruled. "By the staff, Baron von Richter. You, of course, may remain, but dismiss the rest of these men."

Richter's eyes were poisonous as he obeyed. Walking to the doorway with his men, he gave them low-spoken orders. Then he turned to glare at the damning record; stood there uncertainly, as though he debated the advisability of trying to smash it with a bullet.

And then the voice of Franz Schnabel came forth. Incredulously, the staff officers glanced at one another as they began to comprehend the meaning of what they heard.

"—and Bruno Caesar knows—that is the finest part of it," the guttural, recorded voice was chuckling. "He thinks our armies are ready to sweep across Belgium and Holland and throw a scare into England—but the moment I give the word they will storm through the Brenner Pass, while our bombers fly machine-gun units into the very heart of the country. In less than a week Italy will be ours from one end to the other—and then all Europe will be at our feet!"

Gasps of stunned amazement, of fierce rage, escaped from the absorbed listeners as they stared at that revolving disk. Their eyes kindled with fury as they realized how they had been tricked.

"Germany, the undisputed master of Europe, from the Arctic to the Mediterranean, with all the resources of the American continent at our command," the dictator's voice gloated at them; "that will be world dominion, my dear von Richter!" But Marshal Rinaldi had heard enough. Convinced at last, he whirled to confront Richter—only to find that the German had quietly slipped from the tent.

"General Abruzzi, give orders to have the offensive stopped immediately," Rinaldi turned to one of his officers.

"You, Major Sansevero," he instructed another, "see that the American prisoners are released and have their arms restored. And you, Colonel Di Carlo—I want Baron von Richter and his agents placed under arrest."

The offensive was stopped... America was saved!

Operator 5 hardly heard the rest, as the full measure of his success came home to him.

The invasion was at an end—nothing else mattered. He hardly heard Rinaldi's apologies and thanks. It was all like a wondrous, almost unbelievable mirage—until Colonel Di Carlo stood there in the headquarters doorway, white-faced and grim.

His announcement halted them.

"I could not arrest Baron von Richter, sir," he reported. "He has taken refuge with the German troops—and we are practically prisoners!"

That was the bombshell.

CHAPTER 14
BLOOD WILL TELL

KURT VON RICHTER had acted swiftly the moment he realized that he could no longer prevent Rinaldi from learning of Franz Schnabel's true plans. Slipping out of the marshal's headquarters, he had hurried to the section of the front under the command of General Gustav Woerful—the section where the dread German *flammenwerfen* were working. The Americans were retreating.

When the marshal and the remaining members of his staff stepped out of the headquarters tent to investigate Colonel Di Carlo's astounding announcement, they found the Germans in control of the situation.

The hill to which they had withdrawn not only commanded the ground over which the retiring Italians were streaming, but it practically cut off Rinaldi—his headquarters at the tip of a wide V—from his own troops.

Although the Germans were outnumbered nearly ten to one, Kurt von Richter was the master, Marshal Rinaldi almost a prisoner!

That situation could not last, Operator 5 saw at once. The Italian troops, as soon as they understood what had happened, would be able to surround the hill, close in and attack the German flanks and rear as well as the front. Cut off from his supplies, Woerful could not hope to hold out for more than a few hours....

But Richter had taken all that into consideration—and also

157

taken care of it in his own methodical, ruthless way. Suddenly, the ranks of the Germans opened in dozens of places, and out through the gaps came swarming Dr. Oliver's black-uniformed renegades, with the professor himself in the lead; came rushing down the hill—but not of their own volition.

Jimmy Christopher stared in amazement—and dawning horror! What he thought he saw couldn't be happening—not in the civilized Twentieth Century! *But it was!*

Each of those men had his arms bound tightly at his sides—and lashed against the belly of each of them was a dynamite bomb, its lighted fuse sputtering off the remaining seconds of his life! Human bombs, they rushed wildly toward the ranks of the Italians, prodded on their way by German bayonets and kept running by German bullets that whistled past their ears and sank into their backs!

The utter barbarity of that fiendish expedient appalled Jimmy. Such a ghastly doom was shocking, even for renegades such as these.

And then his heart seemed to stand still, the blood to coagulate in his veins!

"Testa della Madonna!" Rinaldi gasped. *"The poor figlie!"*

The poor young women! There in the front rank of those doomed bomb-carriers came Diane Elliot and Nan Christopher! Their faces ashen with terror, they stared down aghast at the sputtering fuses that were melting away before their helpless eyes!

For a horrible moment Jimmy Christopher stood there like a statue, too appalled to move a muscle—until something seemed to snap in his brain. It galvanized him into frantic action. Like a sprinter leaving the mark, he leaped away from in front of the headquarters tent and raced to meet those death carriers.

Diane or Nan—which should he save, if he could save either of them? That terrible question flashed into his brain as his feet pounded over the turf. Nan, the loyal twin with whom he had spent his whole life—or Diane, the loving fiancée with whom he was pledged to spend the rest of his years, once America was rehabilitated and safe from the greedy clutches of power-hungry dictators? Nan or….

At that moment Diane recognized him, and almost took the decision out of his hands.

"No, Jimmy—no!" she screamed wildly. "You can't save us! You will only throw your own life away! Please, Jimmy—*go back!*"

Frantically, she turned and ran away from him. A groan of sheer agony burst from Jimmy's lips as he called on his straining muscles for a still greater effort. In mid-stride he reached Nan, caught her as she tried to dart away from him, and grabbed that sputtering fuse stem—to tear it clear of the dynamite. Without slackening his pace he was past her, was overhauling Diane, to clutch at her shoulder, whirl her around—and then pitch to the ground with her body locked close in his arms, smothering that hissing fuse against his chest.

Now the black-uniformed death messengers were going down on all sides. The ground shook and the air echoed with the thunder of those ear-splitting blasts. Right and left men were being blown into ghastly mincemeat as they vainly begged for help from those who ran from them in terror.

Momentarily, Jimmy Christopher expected that he and Diane would meet the same fate. Momentarily, he expected one of the doomed men to reach them just as the lighted fuse reached the detonating cap.

Helpless there on the ground, he sheltered Diane as well as he could, covered her with his own body—and belt her soft lips on his cheek.

"It won't be so bad—this way, Jimmy," she whispered. "I was so afraid, but now with you—"

"*Back! Back! Back!*"

The sound of her voice was drowned out by a wild yell that seemed to chant from thousands of throats, and now the ground trembled anew under the pounding tread of a host of feet. Jimmy turned his head and glanced in the direction of that clamorous uproar—and thrilled to as madly courageous a charge as history ever had seen!

OUT FROM the ranks of the Italians came the American prisoners Major Sansevero had released, and at their head raced a man in the uniform of an Italian lieutenant-general—Daniel Porter! Straight into the ranks of those human bombs they charged with leveled bayonets—to seize the black-uniformed wretches, whirl them around and send them racing back whence they had come!

The exploding dynamite played havoc with that gallant band, but they accomplished their desperate purpose. Their flashing bayonets were even more terrifying to Oliver's renegades than the death sputtering at their own bellies. In terror-stricken panic they hesitated—and then ran blindly into the ranks of the now thoroughly panicky Germans.

Utter confusion ruled that field of death. Frantically, men flung themselves to the ground, dived beneath corpses, hid behind one another or ran in any direction in their frenzied attempts to get away from those exploding bombs. A ghastly game of blind man's bluff—with Death looking on and applauding as each new victim was counted out!

Utter confusion—and into the midst of it charged the reformed ranks of the new America, General Ferrara's tatterdemalion army! With bugles blowing and flags flying, they swept across the field they had so lately lost—and at their head ran a youth who yelled, "Jimmy! Jimmy!" while tears ran unashamed down his cheeks.

Tim Donovan was coming to report to Operator 5!

For a moment, Jimmy Christopher knelt beside Diane, his fingers busy at her waist. Then his lips touched hers, clung for a brief instant, and he was at Tim's side, leading that irresistible charge into the ranks of the demoralized Germans. Right through them the berserk Americans tore, driving them in every direction, while Operator 5's keen eyes searched everywhere for a hate-contorted face.

Barely in time he spied his man.

Racing wildly from the blood-soaked field, Kurt von Richter sprang at a young German Uhlan and dragged him from his horse; murdered him with a treacherous bullet when he tried to resist. Eagerly, Richter leaped into the saddle, spurred the horse cruelly, and bent low over its neck as it streaked for the north—and to safety.

Jimmy Christopher's guns were empty when he glimpsed that cowardly get-away—but he still had a paper of matches and the dynamite bomb he had cut from around Diane's waist. Instantly, a lighted match was at the short fuse and his arm arced back, held the bomb a perilous moment—then sent it arrowing at the escaping horseman.

Straight and true that bomb went. Jimmy saw it strike the German secret service chief on the right shoulder—and then the thing that had been Kurt von Richter was ripped into a thousand bloody pieces that mingled with the remains of the poor animal he had commandeered....

Pale and shaken, now that the thing which he had so grimly resolved was accomplished, Operator 5 walked back over the horror-strewn battlefield, to where his sister Nan knelt with Dan Porter's head pillowed in the hollow of her arm.

Porter looked up hesitantly—and now the petulance was gone out of his face, the cynicism from his eyes.

"That charge was the finest thing I ever witnessed, Dan." Jimmy bent over him, shook his hand—and two bright red spots glowed in Porter's blood-drained cheeks.

"It was the least I could do—after what I had done," he said weakly. "I thought I could be a traitor—thought I could avenge myself against my country for slighting me—but I couldn't go through with it. Every man I saw seemed to despise me—but not half as much as I despised myself. I realized then what I had lost, Operator 5. My home, my friends, my honor, my self-respect—and any chance I might have had with Nan. So… there was nothing to do… but to come back.…"

The last words were barely whispered, and then the handsome head fell back in Nan's arm, as her tears splashed down into the dead face—and cleansed it of the last stigma that remained.

As Operator 5 looked down upon the man who once had been a gallant soldier he remembered another brave fighter, back in the days of the Revolution, who had turned his coat because his country did not seem to appreciate the value of his services—and he was thankful that, unlike Benedict Arnold, Daniel Porter had found a way to come back, even though it meant redeeming himself with his own life.…

IT IS a matter of history how Marshal Vittorio Rinaldi's legions pursued the fleeing Germans into Canada and annihilated most of them before marching back to the coast and reembarking for the Italy from which they had been guilefully lured.

"The invasion is over, and I am glad," he confessed to Operator 5 as he shook hands in farewell. "My heart was never in it—especially since that noon when you saved me from an uncomfortable swing over the roofs of Munich! For that, if nothing else—I am glad that you succeeded and that your troubles are over."

Over? Jimmy Christopher wished that they were, but he knew that this was not the end. For, even though he had made a friend of Marshal Rinaldi and made peace with the Italians, there were still the Japanese to be settled with—and the Germans. Whether or not Franz Schnabel had by that time succeeded in his plan to establish himself as the dictator of all Europe, it was far from likely that he would forgive this defeat or relinquish the idea of a "colony" in America.

The end was not yet—and only by constant vigilance, Operator 5 knew, could the sons of the land of liberty be sure of their heritage!

AUTHOR'S NOTE: Exactly how accurate was Operator 5's prophecy was clearly proved within the space of a few short, crucial months when America, scarcely recovered from her desperate defense of her great Line, found herself plunged into the midst of the fiercest ordeal she had yet experienced—a war to the death launched by Asia's wily hordes and instigated, as historians believe, by a still vengeful Germany. The account of this dramatic and thrill-packed era will be found, graphically described, in the next installment.

THE SPIDER

- ❏ #1: The Spider Strikes — $13.95
- ❏ #2: The Wheel of Death — $13.95
- ❏ #3: Wings of the Black Death — $13.95
- ❏ #4: City of Flaming Shadows — $13.95
- ❏ #5: Empire of Doom! — $13.95
- ❏ #6: Citadel of Hell — $13.95
- ❏ #7: The Serpent of Destruction — $13.95
- ❏ #8: The Mad Horde — $13.95
- ❏ #9: Satan's Death Blast — $13.95
- ❏ #10: The Corpse Cargo — $13.95
- ❏ #11: Prince of the Red Looters — $13.95
- ❏ #12: Reign of the Silver Terror — $13.95
- ❏ #13: Builders of the Dark Empire — $13.95
- ❏ #14: Death's Crimson Juggernaut — $13.95
- ❏ #15: The Red Death Rain — $13.95
- ❏ #16: The City Destroyer — $13.95
- ❏ #17: The Pain Emperor — $13.95
- ❏ #18: The Flame Master — $13.95
- ❏ #19: Slaves of the Crime Master — $13.95
- ❏ #20: Reign of the Death Fiddler — $13.95
- ❏ #21: Hordes of the Red Butcher — $13.95
- ❏ #22: Dragon Lord of the Underworld — $13.95
- ❏ #23: Master of the Death-Madness — $13.95
- ❏ #24: King of the Red Killers — $13.95
- ❏ #25: Overlord of the Damned — $13.95
- ❏ #26: Death Reign of the Vampire King — $13.95
- ❏ #27: Emperor of the Yellow Death — $13.95
- ❏ #28: The Mayor of Hell — $13.95
- ❏ #29: Slaves of the Murder Syndicate — $13.95
- ❏ #30: Green Globes of Death — $13.95
- ❏ #31: The Cholera King — $13.95
- ❏ #32: Slaves of the Dragon — $13.95
- ❏ #33: Legions of Madness — $12.95
- ❏ #34: Laboratory of the Damned — $12.95
- ❏ #35: Satan's Sightless Legion — $12.95
- ❏ #36: The Coming of the Terror — $12.95
- ❏ #37: The Devil's Death-Dwarfs — $12.95
- ❏ #38: City of Dreadful Night — $12.95
- ❏ #39: Reign of the Snake Men — $12.95
- ❏ #40: Dictator of the Damned — $12.95
- ❏ #41: The Mill-Town Massacres — $12.95
- ❏ #42: Satan's Workshop — $12.95
- ❏ #43: Scourge of the Yellow Fangs — $12.95
- ❏ #44: The Devil's Pawnbroker — $12.95
- ❏ #45: Voyage of the Coffin Ship — $12.95
- ❏ #46: The Man Who Ruled in Hell — $13.95
- ❏ #47: Slaves of the Black Monarch — $13.95
- ❏ #48: Machineguns Over the White House — $13.95
- ❏ #49: The City That Dared Not Eat — $13.95
- ❏ #50: Master of the Flaming Horde — $13.95
- ❏ #51: Satan's Switchboard — $13.95
- ❏ #52: Legions of the Accursed Light — $13.95
- ❏ #53: The City of Lost Men — $13.95
- ❏ #54: The Grey Horde Creeps — $13.95
- ❏ #55: City of Whispering Death — $13.95
- ❏ #56: When Thousands Slept in Hell — $13.95
- ❏ #57: Satan's Shakles — $14.95
- ❏ #58: The Emperor From Hell — $14.95
- ❏ #59: The Devil's Candlesticks — $14.95
- ❏ #60: The City That Paid to Die — $14.95
- ❏ #61: The Spider at Bay — $14.95
- ❏ #62: Scourge of the Black Legions — $14.95
- ❏ #63: The Withering Death — $14.95
- ❏ #64: Claws of the Golden Dragon — $14.95
- ❏ #65: The Song of Death — $14.95
- ❏ #66: The Silver Death Reign — $14.95
- ❏ #67: Blight of the Blazing Eye — $14.95
- ❏ #68: King of the Fleshless Legion — $14.95
- ❏ #69: Rule of the Monster Men — $16.95
- ❏ #70: The Spider and the Slaves of Hell — $16.95
- ❏ #71: The Spider and the Fire God — $16.95
- ❏ #72: The Corpse Broker — $16.95
- ❏ **NEW:** #73: The Spider and the Eyeless Legion — $16.95

THE WESTERN RAIDER

- ❏ #1: Guns of the Damned — $13.95
- ❏ #2: The Hawk Rides Back from Death — $13.95
- ❏ #3: Gun-Call for the Lost Legion — $13.95
- ❏ #4: The Law of Silver Trent — $13.95
- ❏ #5: The Gun-Prayer of Silver Trent — $13.95
- ❏ #6: Silver Trent Rides Alone — $13.95

G-8 AND HIS BATTLE ACES

- ❏ #1: The Bat Staffel — $13.95

CAPTAIN SATAN

- ❏ #1: The Mask of the Damned — $13.95
- ❏ #2: Parole for the Dead — $13.95
- ❏ #3: The Dead Man Express — $13.95
- ❏ #4: A Ghost Rides the Dawn — $13.95
- ❏ #5: The Ambassador From Hell — $13.95

DR. YEN SIN

- ❏ #1: Mystery of the Dragon's Shadow — $12.95
- ❏ #2: Mystery of the Golden Skull — $12.95
- ❏ #3: Mystery of the Singing Mummies — $12.95